A Billy Buckhorn Supernatural Adventure

PARANORMAL

by Gary Robinson

7th Generation
Summertown, Tennessee

7th Generation, an imprint of
Book Publishing Company
PO Box 99, Summertown, TN 38483
888-260-8458
bookpubco.com
nativevoicesbooks.com

ISBN: 978-1-939053-08-4
20 19 18 17 16 15 1 2 3 4 5 6 7 8 9

Library of Congress Cataloging-in-Publication Data

Robinson, Gary, 1950-
Paranormal : a Billy Buckhorn supernatural adventure / Gary Robinson.
pages cm. -- (Billy Buckhorn supernatural adventures ; 2)
Sequel to: Billy Buckhorn : abnormal.
ISBN 978-1-939053-08-4 (pbk.) -- ISBN 978-1-939053-95-4 (e-book)
1. Cherokee Indians--Oklahoma--Fiction. [1. Cherokee Indians--Fiction. 2. Indians of North America--Oklahoma--Fiction. 3. Supernatural--Fiction. 4. Spirits--Fiction. 5. Monsters--Fiction. 6. Family life--Oklahoma--Fiction. 7. Healers--Fiction.] I. Title.
PZ7.R56577Par 2014
[Fic]--dc23
2014018161

Book Publishing Company is a member of Green Press Initiative. We chose to print this title on paper with 100% postconsumer recycled content, processed without chlorine, which saved the following natural resources:

- 18 trees
- 563 pounds of solid waste
- 8,414 gallons of water
- 1,551 pounds of greenhouse gases
- 8 million BTU of energy

For more information on Green Press Initiative, visitgreenpressinitiative.org. Environmental impact estimates were made using the Environmental Defense Fund Paper Calculator. For more information visit papercalculator.org.

CONTENTS

THE CONTINUING ADVENTURES OF BILLY BUCKHORN

Billy Buckhorn's exciting story begins in *Abnormal*, when Billy's supernatural abilities become enhanced and he uncovers a frightening secret about an evil teacher's past. After *Paranormal*, the suspension mounts further, as Billy is faced with even greater challenges in *Supranormal*, during which he confronts the dark force that has spread across the Cherokee Nation. Watch for additional volumes in the Billy Buckhorn Supernatural Adventures series, coming soon!

NOTE TO READERS

O-si-yo (hello). As I noted in *Abnormal*, this is a work of fiction. However, in the interest of realism, I've blended true elements of Cherokee culture and history with made-up information. Some parts have been adapted to protect the privacy of certain medicine people and their practices. Others have been invented to create a more interesting and dramatic story. I point this out so some readers won't dismiss the book because it lacks cultural accuracy. And so that other people won't think I am revealing Cherokee secrets that shouldn't be revealed. *Wa-do* (thank you).

—*Gary Robinson*

paranormal: beyond the range of normal experience or scientific explanation, including such phenomena as ghosts, psychic abilities, and communication with spirits.

CHAPTER 1
Down the River

Eastern Oklahoma's crisp autumn air always reminded sixteen-year-old Cherokee Billy Buckhorn of his grandma Awinita. The Cherokee medicine woman usually served hot apple cider and warm pumpkin pie whenever he went to visit her and Grandpa Wesley in the fall months. Sadly, she passed away when Billy was only six years old. But he continued to smell the sweet aroma of apple cider and pumpkin pie at odd times and places during the season.

Like this morning when he woke up inside his tent on the bank of the Arkansas River. He and his best friend, Chigger, were on a canoeing and camping trip. It would take them along this wide, winding river for the four-day Thanksgiving break. Chigger lay in his sleeping bag on the other side of the tent a few feet from Billy—snoring.

The odors that Billy expected to smell in that tent that morning included his own stinky feet, sweaty camping clothes, stale potato chips, and decaying fallen leaves that lay near their camp. But not apple cider and pumpkin pie.

Then Billy realized it was probably just his mind playing tricks on him. After all, it was Thanksgiving Day. Many families would be starting to prepare the day's big meal. That could include baking pumpkin pies in the oven and warming up apple cider on the stove. So his own memories of Thanksgiving Days gone by might have produced the strong smells in his brain.

It hadn't been all that hard for the boys to convince their parents to let them go on this trip instead of staying home for the holiday. Billy's dad was usually carrying on about the "myth of the first Thanksgiving." He said the Pilgrims never really invited the Indians over for dinner to thank them for helping them survive. So the Buckhorn family often didn't do much that day. Sometimes Billy's mom worked at the hospital during the holiday to earn extra money for the family. That's what she'd be doing today.

Chigger's parents, Sam and Molly Muskrat, needed to spend most of the four days fixing several leaks in the roof of their aging mobile home. The last storm that blew into Cherokee country had ripped loose several roof sections. The next storm would bring damaging rains that would ruin carpets and furniture unless those leaks were sealed. Luckily, Chigger had escaped from these home-repair duties.

Billy unzipped his sleeping bag and checked the portable thermometer hanging from the tent's center support pole. It read thirty-two degrees. That was warmer than the TV weatherman had predicted. Grabbing his camouflage coat, the brown-skinned boy crawled out of the tent to greet the frozen morning. He already had on his clothes because he'd worn them to bed the night before.

Rays of sunlight fell on his face, and he smiled.

"Good morning, Grandfather Sun," he said in English. Then he repeated the greeting in Cherokee. He could see the fog of his warm breath in the chilly air.

Picking up a few dried twigs and dead leaves from the pile that he and Chigger had collected yesterday, Billy set about the task of building a fire. He started by arranging the kindling in the shape of a little tipi in their fire pit. He struck a match and touched the flame to the base of the small leaf-and-twig building to get a fire going.

His grandpa Wesley liked to joke that traditional Cherokees used only "traditional Cherokee matches" to light fires, like their ancestors had done in the old days. Of course, there was no such thing as a traditional Cherokee match. And traditional Cherokees often used the best and easiest method they could find to do things.

After adding a few larger pieces of wood to the fire, Billy performed the seven directions ceremony Grandpa Wesley had taught him. He hadn't missed a morning since his dangerous clash with the Raven Stalker a couple of months earlier.

He honored the four directions—east, south, west, and north—for the wisdom and strength each brought to him. Then he honored Father Sky above him and Mother Earth beneath him for their life-giving energies. Finally, he honored his own heart, his own being—a gift given by Creator, who was the source of it all.

When he'd finished, he could still smell the apple cider and pumpkin pie. It was a comforting smell, so he decided to stop questioning it. He just accepted it. After all, it *was* better than smelling those other odors he'd thought of.

Then he decided to play a little trick on his friend. Moving quietly toward the tent where Chigger still lay sleeping, Billy roared like a bear and pawed at the sides. Inside,

Chigger abruptly sat up and yelled at the top of his lungs. He feared for his very life. At that point Billy howled with laughter at his friend's frightened response.

Chigger sighed at once again being pranked by his old friend.

"You got me good, Billy," Chigger said as he stumbled out of the tent. He was pulling on his own army-surplus coat. "And I was having this great dream about hot apple cider and warm pumpkin pie."

That took Billy by complete surprise.

"That's weird, because I've been smelling those very things since I woke up," Billy said. "But I just thought my mind was playing tricks on me."

"Speaking of pie and cider, what's for breakfast?" Chigger asked, though he already knew the answer.

"Whatever we can shoot or catch," Billy said. "Do you want to go hunting or fishing this morning?"

"How about a quick trip to McDonald's?" Chigger joked. "Do they have a paddle-through window?"

"Out here all you could get is an order of flies and a chocolate snake," Billy said as he joined in the joke.

As the boys chuckled at their own brand of humor, Billy grabbed the coffeepot and bag of ground coffee.

"I'll start some coffee," Billy said. "You look like you could use a cup."

Chigger ducked back inside the tent briefly. When he came back out he was holding two large protein bars wrapped in shiny packages.

"Or we could just chow down on these," he said.

He handed one of the bars to Billy. He was proud that he'd brought something Billy hadn't.

"I thought we were going all natural on this outing," Billy said as he tore open the wrapping on his bar. He took a bite.

"That was your big idea," Chigger said, taking a bite out of his own bar. "I never agreed to any such thing."

The two friends squatted by the fire. Warming themselves and watching the coffee boil, they chewed on their breakfast.

"Chigger, I'm sorry I haven't had more time to spend with you lately," Billy said between bites. "It's just that—"

"I know, I know," Chigger interrupted. "Since you hooked up with Sara, you don't have time for anything or anyone else. That's the problem!"

"I didn't realize that girlfriends demanded so much time and attention," Billy said in his own defense. "It's a new experience for me. And I do enjoy being with her."

"More than doing things with me, I guess," Chigger replied.

Rather than answer, Billy poured them both a cup of the freshly brewed black coffee.

"Don't make this a you-against-her thing," Billy said. Handing his friend a cup, he added, "I've only known her for two months now.

You and I have been pals all our lives. And as far as I'm concerned, we always will be."

Chigger sipped and chewed quietly for a long moment. Billy's vow of lifelong friendship had begun to soothe his hurt feelings.

"Okay, I accept your apology," Chigger finally said, standing up. "But don't think this little trip completely makes up for ignoring me." He turned and headed for the tent.

"I swear, Charles Checotah Muskrat, you sound more like my girlfriend than my girlfriend!" Billy called out.

Chigger stopped dead in his tracks, turned, and made a running dive at Billy. Hitting his mark, the two boys wrestled and rolled not far from the fire.

"Hey, hey, hey," Billy protested as he wrestled. "You'll get us both burned!"

Chigger released his hold and fell on his back. The boys broke out laughing. That felt good to them both. The tension that had been hanging over them had dissolved.

Soon they became totally focused on the day's adventure.

The sun was still low in the sky as they broke down camp and cleaned up the site. Quickly their gear was packed away and stowed. With one last check of the campsite, the pair stepped into their canoe and shoved off shore.

They moved easily downstream. Because they were following the flow of the river, they really didn't have to work that hard. This river flowed south and east through Oklahoma. Then it passed through Arkansas and spilled into the Mississippi River. All that water was headed for the Gulf of Mexico.

But the boys weren't going that far. They were only going as far as the state line. If they felt like it. There was really no set place to get to. This trip was more about the journey itself. Exploring for the sake of exploring.

As the day moved along, so did the river. It took them through several changes in landscape and scenery. Plowed fields, jagged bluffs, majestic oaks, and sandy shorelines cruised by. The sun rose in a cloudless sky, warming the air to a pleasant sixty degrees. That's what Billy's thermometer read. At midday, they fished from the canoe as it floated along. Chigger used a cane pole he'd brought. Billy tried his hand at gigging.

A gig was a long pole tipped with a fork-like spear. Billy learned from Grandpa Wesley that the Cherokees had used them a lot in the old days. Gigs were good for harvesting fish, frogs, and lizards to eat. Billy was almost as good with a gig as he was with a blowgun. Chigger remembered that his friend had won first prize in the blowgun contest during the Cherokee National Holiday in September.

Billy successfully speared three fish and Chigger pulled in two. So they stopped at a curve in the river to cook their meal. Finding a sandy shore, they built a small fire using dried driftwood. To the main course they added dried fruit and nuts they'd brought from home.

Before shoving off again, they checked the map to see what might be coming up ahead. Billy's dad, the college professor, had told him of ancient Native burial grounds near Spiral, Oklahoma. The site had once been home to the original peoples of the area. They created cities a thousand years ago that were larger than cities in Europe at the time.

Billy found Spiral Mounds State Park on the map. It seemed to be a little farther down river than the boys wanted to go. Chigger spotted a section of the river that looked interesting. It was closer to them. And it seemed to be away from homes, farmland, and towns. That was just what they were looking for. They decided to shoot for that spot before nightfall.

The afternoon shadows grew long as the sun set in the west. The boys had to do some real paddling to keep on schedule. It would be no fun trying to set up camp in the dark.

Before long, they arrived at the stretch of river they were looking for. A rugged, rocky shore rose straight up from the water's edge for about one hundred yards. Lucky for them, a shelf of flat land jutted out from the cliffs ahead. It was just large enough for a campsite, with room for a fire pit. There was also room for the tent and a parking place for the canoe.

The boys stepped out of the canoe and onto the shore. They were surprised when the sweet smell of apple cider and pumpkin pie washed over them. They looked at one another with question marks in their eyes. What the heck was going on?

CHAPTER 2
The Crystal Cave

The boys didn't have time to dwell on the issue very long. It was rapidly growing dark in their overnight river-canyon home. They quickly set about the task of unloading the canoe and making a camp. Because they'd done this so many times over the years, it didn't take them long to get set up.

By the time night fell, they had food cooking over the open fire they'd built. This time the food came from freeze-dried food packs furnished by Chigger. They weren't as tasty as wild rabbit or fresh fish, but they didn't require catching or skinning. Chigger was once again proud that he'd thought of bringing something Billy hadn't thought of.

After they'd eaten their freeze-dried chicken-fried steaks and mashed potatoes,

Billy launched into a history lesson he'd learned from this dad.

"What do you know about the Mound Builder Indians, Chig?" he began.

"Not much," Chigger replied. "We had a couple of pages on them in my American History class last year. In the part about prehistoric America. But I don't remember school stuff when I'm not in school. Heck, I hardly remember it when I'm *in* school."

"*Mound Builders* is the name for one group of Indians who lived in villages near the rivers long ago. They had big, permanent towns that stretched out for miles. Over time those Natives became the tribes we know today."

"How do you keep this stuff in your head? Is it part of what your dad taught you?"

"Yeah, but I'm kind of into learning where things came from. What was around before we came along, you know?"

"Sure," Chigger said with a "whatever" attitude. He wasn't big on lectures about some old piece of historic trivia.

"Anyway," Billy resumed, "about a thousand years ago, Mound Builders began building large earthen mounds. These were places where the chiefs and priests lived. The chiefs ruled over thousands of people. The priests led large numbers of religious followers who carried out their every command."

Chigger yawned a big, loud yawn meant to shut down Billy's lecture before it went any further. But Billy kept on.

"One of those Mound Builder towns was located just down the river from where we are now, at Spiral," he continued.

Chigger began snoring loudly, as if he'd fallen asleep.

"Okay, okay," Billy said. "I get the message. But you're missing an interesting bit of Native American history."

Chigger made big, loud gestures of moaning, smacking his lips, and scratching his head to prevent Billy from saying another word. Chigger's dramatic actions were successful. Billy agreed to call it quits for the night.

They remembered to do one last thing before curling up in their sleeping bags. That was to check the battery on the satellite phone they'd brought. They kept this special piece of high-tech gear in a waterproof bag. That way it wouldn't get wet if their canoe tipped over.

The tribe's Marshal Service had loaned the device to Billy and Chigger. This was after the boys helped to rescue Sara from the Raven Stalker last September. That's when the tribe learned that neither Billy nor Chigger owned cell phones.

Deputy marshal Travis Youngblood offered to make the boys honorary Youth Marshals, which included a crash course in emergency preparedness. He worked with the boys, and they became friends in a short time. Deputy Marshal Youngblood gave them the phone, known as a "sat phone," as sort of an award for bravery in the face of danger.

What was great about sat phones was that they worked in places a cell phone wouldn't. All you needed was to be out in the open. The phone worked by sending and receiving signals to a satellite circling thousands of miles above the earth. And Deputy Marshal Youngblood had already programmed in his phone number along with several other area emergency service numbers. Call him anytime, day or night, Youngblood had said.

Chigger pulled their phone out of its container and turned it on. He could read both the battery level and signal strength on the unit's LED screen.

"They're both at full strength," he reported. "Sure hope we don't have to use this thing," he added as he shut it off and stuffed it back in the waterproof bag.

"I bet we're the only kids in the Cherokee Nation with a satellite phone," he bragged. "Too bad we can't play video games on it out here in the dark."

"I *could* call Sara on it to say good-night," Billy said.

"I think I'm gonna be sick," Chigger replied with great drama. "All that smoochy talk between you two makes me wanna barf."

He made a grand gesture of gagging himself by the light of the camp lantern. Then the boys fell silent. Though they'd forgotten about it earlier, the boys could still smell the aroma of pie and cider floating on the air.

The night was mostly quiet. The only sound to be heard was river water flowing nearby. The calming noise quickly put the fearless explorers fast asleep.

Billy awoke the following morning with a start. He lay in his sleeping bag and listened to his surroundings. Nothing. He looked across the tent. Chigger's sleeping bag was empty. He was already up and gone.

Billy stepped outside the tent. The morning air felt warmer than it had the previous day. But there was no sign of his friend anywhere in the campsite. This was unusual. Chigger rarely ventured into unknown places without Billy.

But ever since the Raven Stalker incident, Billy's friend had become a little more adventurous. He hadn't been as fearful of doing things alone at night. He hadn't looked to Billy to always take the lead. Maybe this was because Chigger had been forced to do many things alone since the era of Sara began. Or maybe he had grown more courageous. After all, Chigger had played a role in saving Billy's life in the nick of time.

"Chigger!" Billy called out. "Where are you?"

No answer. He searched the camp area for clues to his friend's location. That's when he noticed a piece of yellow cloth. It was tied to a cluster of vines growing up the face of the jagged cliff behind the campsite. He recognized the cloth as part of the trail kit they'd brought with them. The yellow flags could be used to mark a trail in the woods by tying them to trees or shrubs.

Within a few steps, Billy was close enough to the cloth to reach out and touch it. That's when he first noticed a hollowed-out indention in the cliff rock next to the cloth. Just above that indention was another one. And then another one above that. Stepping back and looking up, Billy realized that these were man-made steps cut into the side of the cliff. And they seemed to run up about thirty or forty feet to a ledge that jutted out from the cliff face.

"Chigger, are you up there?"

Again, no answer.

"All right, here I come," he said loudly, half expecting Chigger to jump out from behind a rock or something. But there was nothing for Chigger to hide behind. So up the carved-out staircase Billy went.

When he got to the top step, it was an easy sideways move to reach the ledge he'd seen from below. The ledge stuck out from the cliff far enough for him to safely stand upright. From that viewpoint, he could look out west. He could see across the river and beyond the shorter rocky hill on the other side. Beyond that hill were rows of smaller, tree-covered hills in the distance.

Upstream to his right was the highway bridge they'd paddled under yesterday. Downstream to the left a few miles were the ancient Indian mounds at Spiral.

Turning back to the ledge, he saw Chigger's boot prints in the shallow layer of sand that covered the ledge. Those prints led directly to an opening in the side of the cliff. It was a cave! And Chigger had entered it by himself! Billy was shocked. His timid friend had gone in there alone. He stood at the mouth of the cave and called in.

"Chigger, are you in there?"

To his relief, there was a reply from within the darkness.

"Billy, you gotta see this!" Chigger's excited voice rang out. "It's stupendous!"

"I don't have a flashlight," Billy said. "How can you see where you're going?"

"Hang on," Chigger replied. "I'll bring the light to you."

In a few moments, Billy saw the bouncing beam of a high-powered flashlight coming toward him through the darkness. In another few moments, Chigger's form emerged from that darkness.

"Look at you," Billy said when his friend reached him. "Exploring a deep, dark cavern all by yourself."

"Different, huh?" Chigger said with a big grin. "Wait till you see what I found. This way."

He turned the light back toward the darkness. He walked down a narrow path that led deep into the cave. Billy followed. As the pair moved inward, the light from outside faded behind them. Soon they were engulfed in a black velvet blanket pierced only by the light in Chigger's hand.

Strange shapes and alien forms surrounded the teens. These were revealed as the flashlight's beam glanced over the cave's inner surfaces. Stalactites hung from the cave's ceiling. Stalagmites grew upward from the uneven floor. These mineral structures looked like pairs of frozen arms reaching toward each other.

Ahead, Chigger and his light came to a stop.

"This is what I wanted you to see," Chigger called out.

Billy caught up to his friend a moment later. Chigger's light pointed to a place where the path split in two. To the right, the flashlight showed a path leading downward. And to the left there was a path leading upward. Right in the middle where they stood was the edge of a cave wall that separated the two.

"Now look closer," Chigger said, pointing the light at a spot on the dividing wall. Billy stepped closer to the bright spot to see what Chigger was talking about. After his eyes adjusted, a panel of markings and etched drawings came into focus.

"What did I tell you?" Chigger asked proudly. "Is that stupendous or what?"

Billy remained silent as he examined the markings more closely. These were cut into the stone, carved by some sharp object. On the left side of the panel was a crude drawing of what looked like a half man–half bird standing next to some sort of pedestal or altar.

On the right side was another drawing. This time there was a creature that looked like a big snake with antlers, floating underwater. Billy reached out to touch the markings and realized that there was a layer of dust partly covering them. Brushing the dust away revealed two more shallow symbols.

On the right, near the serpent, an arrow pointed to the downward path. Below the arrow was a large X. On the left, near the half man–half bird figure, an arrow pointed upward. It also had an image that looked like a sun coming up over the horizon.

"Well, what are we waiting for?" Billy asked. "Up or down? Which way?"

"I'll let you pick," Chigger replied. "I'm not ready for that kind of pressure."

Billy gave his friend a funny look.

"What are you talking about, Chigger? This is your discovery. You get to choose."

That seemed to make Chigger nervous.

"Okay, let me think about it for a minute." He stood there with a pained look on his face. Billy thought this was ridiculous. He grabbed the light from Chigger's hand, pointed it along the upward path, and headed out.

"Wait for me!" Chigger yelled when he realized he was being left behind.

Within about fifty feet, the boys rounded a corner in their upward climb and came upon an amazing view. The cave opened up into a large space filled with thousands of whitish clear crystals. Some came up from the floor. Others grew out of the walls and the ceiling. These gems jutted this way and that. As Billy moved the flashlight's beam across the crystals, countless numbers of smaller light beams were reflected and refracted in every direction. The resulting light show was dazzling.

"WOW," was all Chigger could say.

"Double WOW," was all Billy could say.

They continued on the upward path through the crystal room. The path eventually curved again and ended in a smaller crystal room. Searching the space with their light beam, they found a raised platform in the middle of the area. It was about four feet tall and looked like the pedestal they'd seen in the markings at the beginning of the path.

Standing upright in the top middle of the pedestal was a large, perfectly shaped quartz crystal. When the light fell on it, smaller beams of light shot out from it in several directions. These refracted beams lit up more drawings on the curved walls surrounding the crystal. Chigger held the flashlight in place while Billy went to investigate the images.

They seemed to be a series of scenes that showed the half man–half bird surrounded by a group of people. The outlines of half of the people were clearly drawn. The outlines of the other half of the people were kind of fuzzy, like they were out of focus or something. Or they might have been ghosts.

"We need a petroglyph expert or someone who can decode what these drawings mean," Billy remarked. "This whole thing is beyond belief."

"We should bring your dad in here," Chigger suggested. "He might know what they mean or at least know somebody who knows."

"Let's go back down to where we started and see where the other path leads," Billy said. "No telling what's down there."

"I don't think that's a good idea," Chigger offered. "There was a big X near the arrow for that path. I think it means don't go there."

"Don't be such a sissy," Billy replied as he took the flashlight and started back down the path. "It might mean X marks the spot where the treasure is hidden."

"I hadn't thought of that," Chigger responded more cheerfully. "Let's go!"

The boys quickly made their way back to the fork in the path and took the one on the right side of the divide. As they moved downward, the cave formations became more gnarled and misshapen. The outcroppings looked a little like melted people of different sizes.

Within a few minutes, the boys came to a section of the path that had become partially blocked by large boulders. The huge rocks looked like they might've fallen from the cave's roof.

"Maybe an earthquake hit this area sometime in the past," Billy suggested.

"Or something is warning us that danger lurks below," Chigger said with a nervous laugh.

"C'mon, Chig, don't be a party pooper," Billy chuckled as he picked his way over the fallen boulders and through the narrow opening.

The path took them in a wide downward spiral along the outer edge of another, lower cavern. This space was shaped like a large barrel lined with beautiful, dark purplish crystals. However, the flashlight's beam was not reflected or refracted by these crystals. Instead, it seemed that the light was fully trapped and absorbed by them.

After a few more rounds of the spiral, the path entered a tunnel that continued downward.

In another twenty yards or so, the boys reached the bottom of the cavern. The tunnel ended at a little flat, open area. It was a dead end. Or was it?

They realized that the wall they faced was actually a door, a large door made of a flat stone.

“The cavern floor must be on the other side of this door,” Billy observed. “I wonder if it can be opened.”

The boys began examining the door and its surroundings more closely. Etched into the surface of the door was another set of symbols, along with a drawing of the same snake with antlers they’d seen earlier. Next to the door stood a pedestal like the one they’d seen in the upper clear-crystal room. But the crystal resting on top of this pedestal was a dark purplish color. And it was much smaller—small enough to fit in your hand. It gave off a dim, eerie purplish glow.

Chigger's curiosity led him to reach out and touch the dark crystal. The glow grew brighter with his touch. Withdrawing his hand, he took a quick backward step.

"What was that about?" Chigger said.

"Beats me," Billy responded. "Do it again, but this time leave your hand on the crystal."

Slowly Chigger reached out and put his hand on the stone. He left it there. The crystal began to once again grow brighter. The longer Chigger's hand remained in place, the brighter it glowed. And it grew warmer the longer he touched it. After a few long seconds, he pulled back from it.

"This is creepin' me out," the boy said, stepping away. As he stepped back, he lost his footing in the loose dirt beneath his boots. To keep from falling, he reached to grab hold of something that would support him. His flailing hand found the dark crystal and pulled on it. Rather than keeping him from falling to the ground, the crystal came loose from the pedestal. Chigger clutched it tightly as he fell to the ground.

Once the crystal left its base, a seal of some sort around the stone door was released. The boys heard a "psssst" and felt a rush of cold, stale air coming from the edges of the door. It moved open a few inches. Waiting to see if anything else was going to happen, the pair remained still and quiet for a long moment.

As Chigger stood up, Billy moved toward the open door. Gently at first, he pushed on the door. Realizing that the heavy stone would need a bigger push, he motioned for Chigger to help him. Together, the boys managed to push the stone door fully open.

Billy shined the flashlight through the opening. He saw that the stone path they stood on extended beyond the door a few feet. Beyond that, his light fell on what he assumed to be the cavern's floor. It appeared to be made of smooth, dark glass.

He cautiously took a few steps through the doorway into the huge cavern, followed by Chigger. Feeling a little brave, Chigger started to step out onto the glassy floor when Billy suddenly thrust out his arm to block him.

"Wait," Billy instructed.

"Why?" Chigger asked.

Without answering, Billy squatted down at the edge of the glass and reached out his hand. When he touched the dark surface, his fingers sunk into it.

"Because it's not a solid floor," Billy said lifting his fingers out again. "It's some sort of liquid." Dark drops of the fluid dripped from his fingers.

"What the—?" was all Chigger could get out.

CHAPTER 3
Medevac

"Okay, I've seen enough," Chigger said in a loud whisper as he backed away from the dark liquid at the bottom of the cavern. "Come on. Let's get outta here."

Billy was still pointing the light across the liquid floor when he thought he saw a ripple in the fluid. Chigger saw it too and gasped.

"Man, I'm tellin' ya, I don't like what I'm seeing!" the boy whispered loudly.

He grabbed the flashlight out of Billy's hand and intended to head back up the path. The flashlight's beam swept across the ceiling of the cavern. Chigger saw a wave of movement ripple over the surface.

"The ceiling just moved," he whispered loudly again. "What's with this place? The ceiling moves. The floor that's not a floor moves. And I think I might've just peed my pants."

Billy grabbed the flashlight back from his terrified friend and pointed it upward. He didn't like what he saw there either.

"The ceiling moved because it's covered with bats," he reported to Chigger. "Let's move up the path as quickly and quietly as we can."

The pair proceeded up the spiral path trying to be as invisible as possible. Billy focused the flashlight on the walkway in front of them. Partway up he noticed that Chigger was still clutching the glowing purple crystal tightly in his hand.

"Are you keeping that thing as a souvenir?" Billy asked.

Chigger was fixated on the colony of bats and the moving liquid. He had forgotten he still had the gem.

"That's a good idea," he replied as he stuck it in the pocket of his pants.

At that moment the boys heard a gurgling, bubbling sound coming from the lake below them. And that was it. That was the moment that sent them over the edge.

"Run!" Billy shouted.

The shout started a very surprising chain reaction that began with the bats. Startled, the flying rodents spread their wings one by one. Dropping from their ceiling perches, they took to flight.

Meanwhile Billy and Chigger were struggling to get up the spiral path. It was covered with loose dirt. Their feet slipped and slid beneath them. This made their progress very slow.

Overhead the bats began to swarm, circling the barrel-like cavern in growing numbers. Their movement created a whirlwind of dank air.

The boys were reaching the fallen boulders that partially blocked the path. Just then the whirling bats broke from their circling pattern. The sound of their flapping wings was deafening. And just as the boys started through the narrow opening, the bats headed for that same narrow opening. Billy was in the lead.

Chigger heard the bats coming from behind him. He managed to duck down and lay flat on the path below the opening. The creatures flew above him. Billy had just stepped through the opening when the bats arrived in full force. He was hit by a barrage of bats. Their talons and teeth tore into his flesh as they passed by him. They weren't trying to harm him. They were merely in a rush to escape the cave, just as the boys were.

To make matters worse, Billy couldn't drop to the ground to get out of their way. The sheer force of their numbers kept pushing him along the path. He was forced to take step after step until he reached the mouth of the cave. Beaten and bloodied by the bats, he stumbled out on the cave's ledge.

Back down the path, Chigger was finally free to stand up. The last of the bat swarm flew past him. Then he ran up the path as fast as the loose dirt would let him.

"Billy, are you all right?" he yelled. "Billy?"

There was no answer. Only the sound of hundreds of bats flying out of the cave. Then a fearful yell came from Billy. But that sound faded quickly away.

When Chigger reached the mouth of the cave, there was no sign of Billy, only droplets of blood on the floor of the ledge. The panicked boy peered over the edge of the ledge toward the ground. There, thirty or so feet below, lay Billy in a bloody heap. Not moving.

"Billy, Billy!" Chigger screamed. He scurried down the cliff steps as fast as he could. Reaching his wounded friend, the boy yelled again.

"Billy, Billy!"

He tried to revive Billy, but couldn't. He put his ear to his friend's chest to see if he could hear a heartbeat. Thankfully, he could—a very weak one. What should he do now? He stood and looked around, trying to make his panicked mind work. Then it came to him.

What would Billy do?

An answer immediately flashed in his mind, and he ran to the canoe parked near their tent. Pawing through one of the backpacks, he came up with the sat phone.

"Hang in there, Billy," Chigger said as he turned the phone on. All the important phone numbers had already been programmed in. He hit the quick-dial number for Travis Youngblood back in Tahlequah. The deputy marshal answered before the third ring. Chigger launched into a high-speed account of where he was, what had happened, and what condition Billy was in.

"You've got to hurry and get some medical help over here," the boy said. "Billy looks bad."

"Okay," Travis said. "Stay calm, and stay near the sat phone in case I need to call you back."

"Hurry!" Chigger yelled as Travis hung up.

Within minutes, the deputy marshal made a top-priority emergency call to a nearby medical helicopter ambulance service. These air ambulances perform what they call a medevac service—short for *medical evacuation.* Within another few minutes, a life-saving team had lifted off from Fort Smith, Arkansas. That's where the closest medevac copter was based.

As he waited, Chigger gripped the sat phone like it was the only thing keeping him sane. After a few long minutes, the phone in his hand rang. It made him jump.

"A medevac copter is on its way," Travis reported. "It could be there in fifteen minutes, Chigger. Just hold on."

While Chigger waited for help to arrive, he dug out the first aid kit and clean clothes. He set about the task of cleaning Billy's wounds and applying pressure to the deeper ones. This he'd learned to do during the marshal's emergency training program. Though his friend had passed out, Chigger talked to him as he worked on him.

"Billy, I'm so sorry this happened to you. It's all my fault. I'm the one who foolishly went into the cave. I never should've done that. Will you ever forgive me?"

After what seemed like an eternity, Chigger heard the sound of helicopter rotors off in the distance. He looked up to see a white helicopter floating above him. The words "Flight Medic" were printed in large letters across the bottom.

Soon two ropes dropped from the craft. Two men quickly slid down those ropes. They were followed by a stretcher in a harness. Stepping back, Chigger let the men get to Billy as soon as possible.

"Marshal Youngblood told us to medevac him to the Indian hospital," one of the medics told Chigger. "But there's not room for you. Sorry."

This was crushing news. Chigger didn't know how he was going to survive not knowing what condition his friend was in. All he could do was watch as the paramedics loaded Billy into the copter. Quickly it zoomed away.

He was left with a lonely silence. Now what was he supposed to do? Thinking it through, he realized he needed to get back home. His father had already planned to pick them up at the nearby highway overpass tomorrow. So he'd need his ride a day early.

He called his own home phone number and explained to his dad what was going on. Without delay, his father jumped in his truck and headed for Chigger's location.

Meanwhile, the Flight Medic copter rushed toward Tahlequah with its human cargo. All the while the paramedics on board watched their patient and kept track of his vital signs. They also called ahead to the hospital to prepare them for their arrival.

When Billy was struck by lightning during Labor Day weekend, his mother, the nurse, was on duty at the hospital. This time she wasn't on duty. So an ER nurse called her at home. She and Billy's father rushed to the

ER as quickly as they could. Grandpa Wesley arrived just a little while later.

Soon the medevac copter touched down on the hospital's helipad. Quickly, the ER personnel rushed to the craft to retrieve their patient. Because Billy had become a local celebrity, they all knew him there at the hospital. The ER doctor in charge of Billy's case, Dr. Jenkins, was a friend of Billy's mom.

Mrs. Buckhorn quickly changed into her nurse's uniform so she could assist in the ER. Billy's father and grandfather were forced to stay out in the waiting room. They were left to worry about what was going on in the emergency operating room.

Once inside the ER, Billy was attached to all kinds of tubes and machines. These were designed to keep him alive and track his vital signs. Dr. Jenkins and his staff moved into high gear. They cleaned his wounds, stitched up his gashes, and pumped him full of medications.

But even though they worked as hard as they could, Billy began slipping away. His heart rate slowed down and got weaker. His brain activity decreased. Dr. Jenkins couldn't understand why this was happening. Billy had suffered a few broken ribs in the fall. But there was really nothing life-threatening about his wounds.

When Billy's heartbeat stopped, the beep-beep-beep sound on the monitor went flat. Then the doctor and his staff switched from high gear to super-high gear. Billy's mother grabbed the paddles that would send electric current into Billy's chest. Dr. Jenkins waited for the machine, called an AED, to charge up.

When it was fully charged, he yelled "Clear!" so that all the other staff would stand back.

Then he applied the paddles to the boy's chest. The paddles, made to shock the heart back into action, zapped electricity into Billy's chest. But Billy's heart did not respond. Maybe because his body had already been shocked by a direct lightning strike, Dr. Jenkins thought.

The doctor repeated the process two more times, again with no response. Sadly, they had to declare Billy Buckhorn dead at 11:45 a.m. on the day after Thanksgiving.

Billy's mother burst into tears.

CHAPTER 4
The Tunnel

No one but Billy knew of the remarkable things he had experienced since he and Chigger had attempted to escape from that cave. The colony of bats swept through the narrow opening. Their wings beat on him furiously as they passed. He threw up his arms and hands to cover his head and face. But their talons and teeth tore into him dozens and dozens of times. The pain Billy felt grew until it became unbearable.

The bats' collective force against his body pushed him ever upward along the path and out on the cave's ledge. Unable to see where he was, he stumbled off the ledge. His own scream was the last thing he remembered hearing. Just before he passed out from hitting the ground, he thought he smelled apple cider and pumpkin pie one last time.

In the darkness, he felt no pain. But he was aware of things around him. Not his earthly surroundings like the camp, the river, or Chigger. Not those things. There was something else in the darkness with him. Something comforting. And that soothing smell of pie and cider.

Suddenly he heard a ripping sound—like two pieces of Velcro being separated. The next thing he realized was that he could see again. And what he saw shocked him. It was like he was hovering a few feet off the ground. Below him was a bloodied body. And that body didn't look like it was in very good condition.

Wait a minute. That was his own body! Lying down on the ground. Not moving.

But for some reason, that didn't bother him. It really seemed like someone else's body. Then the physical body and the ground below him seemed to move further away. He floated upward past the ledge and the mouth of the cave. He literally reached the sky.

That's when he was suddenly pulled at lightning speed away from the river. Soon the view of the land and the sky faded from sight. He began to zoom through a dark tunnel. Up ahead, at the end of the tunnel, he could see a very bright light.

As he got closer to the light, he slowed down. But the light was more than just light. It was full of good feelings. There was a sense of no worries. Like whatever you'd done during your life was not that important. And the smell of pie and cider grew stronger than ever.

Even though he didn't have physical eyes, Billy had to squint in that bright light. He could see the outline of someone nearby. In a few moments, though, he got used to the brightness, or someone dimmed the light. Finally, he could see who was there in the light with him.

"Grandma Awinita?" Billy said. "Is that you?"

"Indeed it is, Grandson," she said. Somehow there was a warm, comforting love coming from her. Billy could actually feel it flow through him. He'd never felt anything like it.

"Where am I?" he asked.

"Somewhere between the land of the living and the land of the dead," she replied. "But you have to understand that the dead aren't really dead. They've left their physical life and simply gone on to another life. A better life. Just like I did when you were six years old."

Billy was confused. He always thought that ghosts were the spirits of the dead, and Cherokees stayed away from ghosts at all costs. The ones he'd heard about weren't very nice. How could that be a better life? These were thoughts he had in his mind but didn't speak.

"I understand your confusion," Awinita replied to his unspoken thoughts. For the first time, Billy realized that she wasn't using her mouth to speak to him. He could read her mind. "Ghosts *are* the spirits of people who were once alive on earth," she continued. "But they got very attached to something or someone. They can't let go and move on into their new life. And they sometimes get angry and confused. So they act out."

"Where does that leave me?" Billy asked.

"You're at a crossroads," the elder replied. Showing Billy an area behind her, she said, "Over there is the border. Cross that barrier and you can't return to your life on earth. That's why I'm here, to help you decide what to do."

"You mean I have a choice?" Billy asked.

"Your entire existence is made of choices. This just happens to be a big one."

Billy waited to hear more.

"You have an unfolding gift that will allow you to do things on earth you never dreamed possible. As your powers increase, you will be able to help people and heal them. And I will give you guidance from this side. So I don't have to worry that you'll ever misuse those powers. I know you won't do things like Benjamin Blacksnake has done."

Hearing that evil name came as a shock to Billy. Everything was so warm and loving, and then BAM! Suddenly Billy felt off balance. He felt like the ground beneath him was about to give way.

"What's it going to be?" his grandma asked. "Willing to go back and fulfill your destiny? Or do you want to end your life on earth and cross over?"

The area behind Awinita glowed with welcoming love and care. And Billy thought he saw a familiar figure step out from the barrier. Was that his great-grandfather, the one called Bullseye Buckhorn? Yes, it was. Billy recognized him from old family photos.

Then he thought of Chigger and Grandpa Wesley back on earth. He wasn't ready to leave them. He was only sixteen years old, after all. He still had a lot of life to live.

"I want to go back," he finally said. No sooner had he thought that thought than he felt another hard-hitting electric shock. BAM!

While recovering from this second one, he began to move away from his grandma and back down the tunnel.

"You made a good choice, Billy," his grandma said with a heart-warming glow. "From now on, you and I will be connected. I will be your helper from this side when you need me. The cider and pie you've been smelling—that's how you'll know I'm around. Do you understand?"

He was nodding his answer when he came out of the tunnel and found himself hovering once again over his own physical body. But it was in a different place. He looked around, trying to figure out where he was. Finally, he saw his mother in her nurse's uniform and realized he was in the Indian hospital.

As Billy watched from above, the doctor placed two large electrical paddles on his physical chest below.

"Clear!" the doctor yelled.

BAM! Billy felt the electric shock in his spirit body for a third time. He was starting to fade out again, drifting back into the blackness.

"Time of death is 11:45 a.m. on November 29," Billy heard the doctor declare, just before he faded into the silent darkness.

The next thing Billy knew, he was gasping for air. It felt like someone was sitting on his chest. He began flailing his arms—his physical arms! Then he opened his eyes, his physical eyes! Dr. Jenkins grabbed one of Billy's arms and his mother grabbed the other. Realizing he was back in his physical body, Billy stopped jerking and gasping.

His eyes came to focus on his mother's face. It was wet with tears that had flowed freely just a few moments ago.

"My boy's alive," she said with great excitement. "It's a miracle!" She hugged him tightly until he complained.

"I can't breathe, Mom," Billy said. "Give me some air!"

She released her grip on her son as the boy looked around the room. Finally, he spotted the person he was looking for.

"Dr. Jenkins, why did you declare me dead?"

This question stunned everyone in the room. They all fell silent. The doctor stepped closer to his patient.

"How did you know I declared you dead?" the doctor asked. "You were . . . well . . . dead."

"I heard you say it plain as day," Billy replied. "I was floating over the room at that moment. I watched everything that happened."

The doctor did not know how to respond to that information. He did not believe this was even possible.

"You had no pulse or heartbeat," he said. "We tried to revive you three times with no success."

Then the puzzled look on his face faded.

"But we're all glad you pulled through, young man," he said with a smile. "Your mother was right. It *is* a miracle. We couldn't bring you back, but somehow you did it yourself."

With their patient revived, the hospital staff scurried around preparing for the next steps of his medical treatment. He was, after all, covered with scrapes, bites, and cuts from head to foot.

And once again, the boy who'd survived a lightning strike, saved a busload of kids, and almost single-handedly brought down a child abuser, was about to begin another chapter in his remarkable life.

CHAPTER 5

What Just Happened?

Billy began recovering nicely from his bat wounds and was allowed to go home three days after he'd been declared dead. His girlfriend, Sara, was among the first to welcome him home.

"I thought I'd lost you forever," she said tearfully as she held on to his bandaged hand. "I don't know what I would've done without my Billy."

What Billy didn't know was that Chigger was standing just outside his room. He heard every word. Billy's mother had met him at the front door and told him he could visit briefly with Billy when Sara left. She was about to leave Chigger at Billy's door, but noticed something odd about the boy.

"You don't look good, young man," she said.

She grabbed his chin and held his face up toward the light. He had dark circles under his eyes. His skin was pale, especially for a full-blood Cherokee.

"I'm just a little tired," Chigger replied. "I've been feeling this way since the day Billy got hurt. I'm sure I'll get over it."

She left him and returned to the kitchen. There she picked up a tray of food and a local newspaper. In a few moments she came back and said, "I'll have Sara out of there in no time."

She moved past Chigger, opened Billy's bedroom door, and entered.

"Here's your lunch," she said. "I want you to eat all of it, too."

Then she turned her attention to Sara.

"Sara, honey, I don't want Billy to get too tired seeing a lot of visitors today. Would you mind coming back tomorrow? You could have another short visit then."

"All right, Mrs. Buckhorn," the girl said. "I need to go home and get on the Internet. I have to update all my online friends about Billy's recovery. You wouldn't believe how many new friends are following me since Billy's hospital miracle!"

Billy had never been a fan of publicity or social media. It bothered him a little that his girlfriend seemed to be so hooked on it. But he didn't say anything. And Billy's mother really wasn't a fan of Sara's either. But she didn't say anything.

To Billy, Sara said softly, "I'll see you tomorrow, my sweet."

Before leaving, she kissed the tip of her own finger and held it up to the lightning scar on the side of Billy's neck. She'd done the same thing back when she first thanked him for saving her life.

Sara was very surprised to find Chigger waiting in the hall. Especially since Mrs. Buckhorn just said she didn't want Billy to have a lot of visitors. It was then that Sara realized that Billy's mother might not be on her side in her battle for Billy's attention.

Sara had originally thought Chigger might be a little bit of a threat to her. Now she was sure of it. But she was also sure Billy would choose her over this scraggly boy.

Sara moved past Chigger without speaking.

"Hello, Sara," Chigger said sweetly with a smile. He knew that he was the winner of this round in the contest for Billy's attention.

"You have two minutes with Billy today," Mrs. Buckhorn announced to Chigger as she left Billy's room.

"Yes, ma'am," Chigger answered.

Stepping into the room, he found Billy studying the newspaper Mrs. Buckhorn had just brought in.

"I thought I'd lost you forever," Chigger said with a mocking sweetness as he batted his eyelashes. "I don't know what I would've done without my Billy." He tilted his head and gave a girlish smile.

"Ha, ha, very funny," Billy said as he looked up from the newspaper. That's when he, too, noticed Chigger's sickly appearance.

"Are you all right, buddy?" Billy asked. "You don't look good at all."

"I'll be fine," his friend replied. "Probably got the flu or something. What's in the newspaper?"

Billy folded the paper over to the story he was reading and handed it to Chigger.

"I managed to get written up in the newspaper again," he said. "You know I hate publicity. Especially this overblown flashy stuff. They make it sound like I can walk on water."

Chigger took the paper and scanned it. The headline read: "Lightning Boy Returns from the Dead." The photo under the headline showed the weblike scars on Billy's neck. These he got from the lightning strike back in September. The story reminded readers of the whole lightning ordeal. And it told of how Billy had used psychic "gifts" to save the busload of children.

What the article didn't report was that those gifts had faded a little over time. He no longer saw flashes of scenes from people's lives when he shook their hands. Nor was he able to learn a whole school lesson by sleeping on a textbook overnight.

What he did keep, though, was the way to speed-read a chapter and remember its most important ideas. And when he met someone, he could "read" them. This told him if they were up to no good.

"My offer still stands," Chigger said with a smile. "I'll be your agent any day. I can get you a reality show and everything." This had become a running joke between the two boys.

He stopped smiling when he saw that Billy wasn't smiling.

"Chigger, I don't think I ever thanked you for saving my bacon once again," Billy said. "If it wasn't for you, I would've died. And I mean *really* died. For good."

Chigger wasn't expecting this at all. He said, "It was nothin'. All I did was make another phone call just like when I found Ravenwood's hideout."

"What you did was use *all* the skills and tools we just learned from the Marshal Service," Billy insisted. "The ER staff told me what a good job you did in cleaning up my wounds down on the river. That's *not* nothing."

"Okay, time's up," Billy's mother announced as she stepped into the room. "Visiting hours are over for today."

Chigger did a fist bump up against Billy's bandaged hand and said, "Thanks, Bro."

"Chigger looks kind of sickly," Billy's mom said when the boy had left. "I'm a little worried about him."

"So am I," Billy agreed.

"He said he started feeling weak the same day as your accident," she added. "Maybe you can convince him to see a doctor. Or pay a visit to Wesley."

"Grandpa is the one person I haven't seen much of since I got home from the hospital,"

Billy complained. "Can you call him for me? I do need to talk to him."

"Okay, I will," Mrs. Buckhorn said. "But right now you need to get some rest. Remember, your uncle John is coming by this evening to bring a get-well message from my side of the family."

She saw an alarmed look cloud Billy's face.

"Don't worry," she said calmly. "He promised not to preach this time."

"But Mom, do I have to?"

"Billy, he's family. He's my brother. Please do it for me."

"Okay—for you," he said in a defeated voice.

"It's like pulling a painful tooth," his mother advised. "Best to just get it over with."

With that she turned out his light and closed the door.

During his afternoon nap, Billy had a nightmare about bats coming at him. Big bats. They grabbed his legs and arms and were about to tear him limb from limb. But then his grandma Awinita appeared nearby. He could smell the apple cider and pumpkin pie. It was like someone turned on a bright light that hurt the bats' eyes. They fled and left him alone with his grandmother.

"Something came out of that cave with you and Chigger," Awinita said within the dream. "Something that's infecting the people of the Cherokee Nation."

Billy awoke with a start. He blinked his eyes and looked around his room. Had his grandma just been there? She must've been. He could still smell a hint of cider and pie. Maybe she was still nearby.

Then he heard his bedroom door creak open a bit. He looked over and saw his mom peeking in. When she saw that he was awake, she opened the door the rest of the way.

"Your uncle is here," she said. "Can he come in?"

"Yeah, I guess so," Billy answered glumly as he sat up in bed.

His mother turned and motioned down the hallway for her brother, the preacher, to come ahead. In a few moments the man, with his slicked-back jet-black hair and tan suit, stepped into the room.

"Don't excite him," Mrs. Buckhorn told her brother. "It's not good for his health."

"Of course not, Rebecca," he replied. "Of course not."

He waited a moment to see if his sister was going to leave the two of them alone. He saw that she wasn't. So he stepped closer to Billy's bed. As he did, the aroma of cider and pie floated into Billy's mind.

"Ah, Billy, it's such a blessing to see you doing so well," John began. "To see you brought back from the brink of the grave. It was the hand of the Lord. Hallelujah, child! Praise God! Like Lazarus whom Jesus called forth from the tomb!"

John continued with his message, but Billy became distracted. A buzzing sound began in his ears. Within that buzzing came a voice. It was weak at first, but as Billy tuned into it more, it grew stronger. Soon he could tell it was Awinita's voice.

"There's someone over here with me who wants to speak to you," she said. "I'm right here, so you don't need to be afraid of it."

Billy nodded in reply to his grandma's statement. Uncle John took that to mean he could keep going with his message. Billy's mother continued to watch to see if her brother's preachy, get-well message was upsetting Billy. Her son seemed surprisingly calm and relaxed.

But Billy barely noticed his preacher uncle's presence. A barely visible scene began to unfold behind the man. It was faint at first. But, like Awinita's voice, it grew stronger as Billy focused on it.

A glowing hole opened in the bedroom wall. A glowing image of Awinita stepped through that hole. With her was a softly glowing American Indian man. Billy understood him to be the spirit of a person once alive on earth. Behind his grandma and this man was something else. There was a cluster of other glowing people who seemed to be waiting for something.

Billy looked to see if his mother or uncle were aware of this golden vision. They didn't seem to be. Then Awinita and the man moved in closer.

"This is your mother's brother, Luther," she said. "That, of course, makes him your uncle, too."

Billy had never heard of an uncle named Luther. The spirit man stepped forward.

"He has a message for his brother and sister at this time," Awinita said.

Billy listened, straining to hear what the spirit man was saying. But Luther wasn't as practiced at speaking with the world of the living as Awinita was. She had been appearing to Billy's grandpa Wesley for years during the Live Oak Stomp Grounds' annual ceremonial dance. So she knew how to do it.

At first Luther's message was no louder than a weak whisper. Awinita's spirit glowed brighter than before. This helped to amplify the strength of his message. Billy could finally hear the man clearly. The boy listened carefully for a brief time. Then Billy relayed the message to his uncle John, and his mother, whose name was Rebecca.

"Luther has given me a message for you, John," Billy blurted out, interrupting the preacher's speech.

At the mention of Luther's name, both John and Rebecca jerked like they'd been slapped in the face.

"What did you just say?" John demanded.

"Luther says you have a lot of nerve preaching to other people about their sins and shortcomings," Billy continued. "He says his life ended because you were arrogant and reckless. Those are his words, not mine."

"How dare you mention that name!" John roared. Then another thought struck him. "How do you even know of him?" he asked. "He died more than twenty-five years ago, and no one in our family has spoken of him since."

"You know Billy speaks the truth," Rebecca said, drawing her brother's attention toward her. "I've never said a word to anyone in all these years, but the truth has been spoken today."

"Answer me, boy," the preacher demanded. He turned his attention back to Billy and stepped closer to him. "What devilry is this?"

"Luther is here now, speaking to me," Billy said calmly, pointing with his lips. "His spirit stands behind you, alongside my grandmother, Awinita."

Both Rebecca and John looked in the direction Billy had pointed. They saw nothing.

"Now I understand," John thundered as he turned back toward his nephew. "This is coming from that devil-worshipping Wesley Buckhorn and his demonic ghost-wife!" He moved ever closer to Billy, his rage building.

Rebecca thrust herself in front of her brother.

"You self-righteous, pompous pretender!" she screamed in his face. Without turning away from John, she spoke to her son.

"Billy, what else did Luther tell you?"

"He said John was in an alcoholic stupor when he got behind the wheel of your father's car. And then he backed over your younger brother, Luther, who was playing at the end of the driveway."

John sharply gasped in a breath of air. So did Rebecca. Together they turned to look at Billy lying in his bed. His face glowed with calm peacefulness.

"Then he blamed the accident on a neighbor he didn't like," Billy said. This completed Luther's message.

John's body grew stiff and his face turned red. Looking as though he might burst, he ran from the room in a state of panic. Billy's mother stood motionless and watched him flee. Moments later, they heard John's car start and speed out of their gravel driveway. Mrs. Buckhorn turned to look at her son who remained calm.

"There are others here with me," Awinita told Billy. "They are waiting for a chance to connect with their loved ones on earth." She pointed to the cluster of waiting souls. "There's no hurry," she added. "But when you are well, you can carry out this work with

Grandpa's help. But only if you want to. Only if you think you can handle it."

Awinita glowed brightly for an instant, smiled, and then faded away. The host of spirits with her faded away, too.

Rebecca stared at her son in awe as she came close to him. She had a million questions and not a clue of how to ask the first one. She lay down quietly on the bed next to him.

"Please tell me what just happened," she softly said at last. "So I can understand."

"I died, and lived to tell about it," her son answered. "And this is part of the reason I came back. To help people connect with their loved ones. To help people with their problems."

And then, for the first time, he told someone the details of what happened in that cave and what happened while he was dead. He had told no one because he feared that people would think he was crazy.

But his mother, the medical-minded nurse, did not think he was crazy.

CHAPTER 6
Heavy Darkness

From that day forward, Billy began to rapidly heal from his many wounds. It was another mystery to Billy's mom and dad.

But at the same time, Chigger's health was rapidly getting worse.

On Saturday, Billy persuaded his mother to allow him to visit both Chigger and his grandpa. Not wanting him to venture out on his own yet, she agreed to the outing only if she drove. The still-bandaged Billy had to agree.

His mother first drove him to Chigger's mobile home a few miles away. Chigger's mother greeted them at her door with a very worried look.

"Today he just won't get out of bed," Mrs. Muskrat told them. "His skin is sickly pale, and he won't eat. And he's in a really bad mood all the time. I've begged to let me take him to a doctor, but he just sort of growls at me."

"That doesn't sound like Chigger at all," Billy said.

"Where's Chigger's father?" Mrs. Buckhorn asked.

"Sam is working a temporary job over in Arkansas," Chigger's mom replied. "He won't be back for a couple of days."

"Can we come in?" Billy asked. "I need to see what's going on with Chigger for myself."

Mrs. Muskrat opened her door and allowed them in. Almost immediately a heavy feeling settled over Billy. He felt tied up, and simply walking became a chore. And the inside of the home seemed dark, even though the drapes were open and the sun shone brightly outside.

"Do you feel that heaviness?" he asked, looking from his mother to Mrs. Muskrat.

Both women shook their heads. They weren't aware of anything like that.

"Please wait out here," Billy said. "I want to see Chigger alone."

As Billy stepped into Chigger's room, the heavy feeling increased. It felt like trying to walk through syrup. And there was a strange odor hanging in the air. Billy couldn't quite place it, but it was kind of sour.

As the teen moved closer to the bed, Chigger slowly turned his head toward him. The ill boy slowly opened his eyes to see who was there. Billy saw Chigger's bloodshot yellow eyes, and he knew his friend was in serious trouble.

"Hey, Chigger," Billy said in a cheery voice. "I've come to see how you're doing."

"I'm surprised Sara let you out of her sight," Chigger said with a weak, gruff voice. "She's got it in for me, you know."

"I'm here now, Chig," Billy replied. "What's going on with you?"

"What's going on is that I'm tired of playing second fiddle to you," Chigger said angrily. "The famous Lightning Boy is adored by everyone. Able to leap tall buildings and come back from the dead."

"You know none of that matters to me," Billy said, taking a few more steps.

"Save that phony-baloney for someone else," Chigger answered sharply. "Fame and glory is what you're really all about. In no time you'll be the most famous Cherokee that ever lived."

As Chigger spoke, his strength grew. His voice took on a deeper, raspier tone. And the yellow in his eyes shifted toward the color purple. Billy hardly knew the figure who now lay in Chigger's bed. His voice and words sounded nothing like the friend Billy had known for more than ten years.

"I can tell you're not yourself today," Billy said. "So I'll leave you alone. Maybe you'll feel better tomorrow."

"Don't let the doorknob hit you in the butt on your way out," the raspy voice said. "And tell that woman who calls herself my mother to leave me alone."

Billy left the room as Chigger began a series of deep, dry coughs.

"Mrs. Muskrat, I think you need to call your husband and get him back here as soon as possible," Billy said once he was back in the living room. "Chigger's illness might make him hard to handle. I mean physically."

Mrs. Muskrat didn't move as she tried to understand what Billy had said.

"And we need to get Grandpa Wesley over here as soon as possible," he said, turning to his own mother. "Chigger isn't just ill. It feels like something's in there with him. Something bad has taken control."

Neither of the two mothers could utter a single word in reply. What Billy was saying didn't seem real. Chigger's mother finally moved to the phone to call her husband.

"We'll be back with my grandpa as soon as we can," Billy said to Mrs. Muskrat while she waited on the phone.

When Billy and his mother got back in the car, she asked, "What was that all about?"

"I don't know for sure," Billy answered. "Something evil is dragging Chigger down."

His mother blinked. "You're beginning to sound like my brother John," she observed and looked at her watch. "I have to start my shift at the hospital soon. Why don't I let you off at your grandpa's house? He can bring you back here later."

Billy agreed, and they drove to Wesley's house. It was located in a remote wooded area north of Tahlequah. Grandpa Wesley had actually learned Cherokee medicine from his wife, Awinita, when they were a young married couple. Wesley carried on after Awinita passed away. That's when he began teaching Billy about Cherokee healing and traditions.

When Billy arrived at Wesley's house, there was a line of Native people waiting on the old medicine man's front porch and in the front yard. Billy had never seen so many people there. *What was going on?*

When the waiting crowd saw the bandaged Billy, a murmur of awe spread among them. They knew of this boy's return from death's door. They also knew of the busload of children he'd saved and the girl he had rescued.

A few of the gathered folks reached out to touch him as he passed. They hoped that he might bless them somehow. Billy did not like this at all. But he just smiled politely and kept heading for his grandpa's front door.

He found Wesley sitting at the kitchen table with mortar and pestle in hand. He was grinding the dried leaves of a medicine plant into small pieces. He looked up from his task.

"What are you doing here, Grandson?" the elder asked. He got up to hug Billy. "Shouldn't you be home getting well?"

"What's going on, Grandpa?" Billy replied with a question of his own. "Why are there so many people needing help?"

"It's been like this for days," Wesley said. He offered his grandson a place to sit. He resumed his task. "They all seem to be suffering from similar problems. They're tired and depressed and angry for no reason. And they've all seen bats near their homes."

That last sentence caught Billy's attention.

"Bats?" he said. "They've seen bats?"

"We hardly ever have bats around here in cooler months," Wesley said. He poured the ground-up herb into a plastic bag. "Now they're everywhere. I don't get it."

"I do," Billy said. "Bats are one of the things we found in that cave. And bats are what gave me these wounds and nearly ended my life. On top of that, Grandma said that something came out of that cave with me and Chigger. Something that was infecting the Cherokee people."

Wesley stopped what he was doing.

"You've seen Awinita again? Even since your near-death experience?"

Billy told him about the bat dream and the visitation from his grandma the previous day.

"That helps to explain why my traditional remedies aren't working as well as they should," Wesley said. He got up and left the room.

Soon he returned with the ancient *Cherokee Medicine Book* that had been recovered from Ravenwood's car in September. This book had once belonged to the Eastern Cherokee medicine man Benjamin Blacksnake. That man had used the book's pages for doing evil. But it also contained much of the tribe's oldest and best healing knowledge.

Wesley placed the book on the kitchen table and began flipping through its pages. Billy only knew a few of the words handwritten there. They were in the Cherokee alphabet. But Wesley could read and understand it all.

"What are you looking for?" Billy asked.

"I sort of remember seeing something about the deeper meaning of bat sightings," Wesley said. "But I don't remember where it is written or what it said."

Near the back of the book, Wesley came to a page that contained several drawings.

"Wait!" Billy shouted just as the elder was about to turn the page. There, in the lower right-hand corner, was an image he'd seen before.

"That's the same picture we saw in the cave," Billy exclaimed. "It was scratched into the rock wall next to the path that led down into the dark cavern."

"Are you sure, boy?" Wesley asked.

"Positive," Billy replied. "What is it and why is it in this book?"

"That's the ancient Horned Serpent," Wesley said in a somber tone. "It is known to the Cherokees as Uktena. These creatures live underwater and have a bright diamond on their foreheads. Legend says that gem could impart great powers to any man who could take it. But all who tried to steal it from the beast died in the process."

"In your teachings about tribal legends, why haven't you told me of this beast before?" Billy asked, still looking at the drawing.

"Because no one has actually seen one for decades, maybe centuries," the elder answered. "Many Cherokee medicine people thought it had gone extinct or never really existed at all."

Then Billy realized something.

"I think I saw one," he said and sat down hard on one of Wesley's wooden kitchen chairs. "At least I may have seen its back. It slithered in the liquid at the bottom of the cave."

He explained how the floor turned out to be some sort of dark liquid instead of a floor. And he told of the ripple of movement he and Chigger saw in that liquid.

Billy finished by saying, "But I thought those cave drawings were done by people of the older Mound Builder culture, not Cherokees. At least that's what Dad told me."

Billy's father was considered the expert in the histories and cultures of Native people of the region. He taught several college classes in these subjects. At times, he'd shared his knowledge with Billy. Billy, in turn, sometimes tried to share this information with Chigger, but usually only succeeded in boring his friend.

"Then we'd better sit down with your dad and put our heads together on this as soon as possible," Wesley said. "Your father doesn't really believe in the teachings of tribal cultures. But he knows more about them than anyone else around here."

Wesley stuck a piece of folded paper in the big book to mark the page where the Uktena drawing could be found.

Then Billy remembered something else.

"I just remembered why I came here," Billy said as his grandpa closed the book. "It's Chigger. He's worse off than any of these people waiting to see you. Can you come with me back to his house?"

"Of course," Wesley replied. "Just let me get my medicine bag and we'll go."

Wesley closed and locked his front door. He explained to those waiting that he had to make an emergency house call to treat someone who was in really bad shape. Being patient people, these Cherokees didn't usually mind an extra wait. They often brought decks of cards or other things to occupy their time.

But today was different. Today they were all suffering from some unknown ailment that made them cranky and impatient. Several of them complained loudly as grandfather and grandson left the house.

Wesley suddenly stopped and turned back toward the crowd. He raised his hands and closed his eyes. Loudly he spoke a paragraph of formal Cherokee in a forceful voice. The sound of his voice speaking those ancient words caused everyone to fall silent.

Wesley finished his words and opened his eyes. He gave the line of waiting people a stern look. Everyone in the crowd seemed to realize how childish they'd been acting. They became embarrassed. Silently they turned their eyes toward the ground.

Satisfied that he'd achieved his goal, Wesley walked to his truck. He and Billy drove away.

CHAPTER 7
Paranormal

Molly Muskrat greeted Billy and Wesley at the door.

"Chigger's father is on his way home and should be here by nightfall," she said as she let them inside. "Mr. Buckhorn, I hope you can help my son. I've never seen him like this. Billy was right. He's not himself."

She waited in the living room as Wesley and Billy entered Chigger's room. The boy was asleep.

"Tell me what you're picking up in here," Wesley said to his grandson. This would be an opportunity for the medicine man to see how much the student had learned. "What does your intuition tell you?"

"There's a heavy darkness all around Chigger. I felt it when I visited with Mom.

Walking feels like trying to move through molasses. The air has a sour smell, too."

"What else?" the elder asked as he moved closer to the boy's bed.

"I feel like something is controlling Chigger from the outside," Billy answered. "It's almost like he's a puppet connected with strings."

"Good read," Wesley said. "There is something more than just a physical illness going on with this young man. He might be under the spell of a Night-Goer. I'll have to take a deeper look to see what's really going on."

Wesley and other medicine men had dealt with Night-Goers before. This was a type of Cherokee witch that usually attacked someone who was already sick. The Night-Goer tried to make the person sicker and sicker to the point of death. The witch wanted to collect the person's internal organs at the time of death, because those fresh organs were a potent source of power.

Wesley took a chair from Chigger's desk in the corner of the room and placed it near the bed. Then he opened his leather medicine pouch. From it he removed a thin, clear quartz crystal. He sometimes used the crystal to help him focus. It improved his ability to "see" into his patients.

He set the crystal down on his knee. Then he pulled a smaller medicine bag out of the pouch and hung it around his neck.

Suddenly Chigger awakened and sat up in bed. His eyes opened wide with anger.

"What is the meaning of this intrusion?" he demanded. The raspy voice was back. "You must leave at once."

It seemed as though Chigger didn't know them at all. The sickly boy squinted and seemed to push outward. Billy then began to feel an unseen force pushing against him. Wesley felt it too, and almost tipped over in his chair. Getting to his feet, he stumbled backward.

"What is that?" Billy asked. "It's becoming very hard to breathe in here."

"Chigger has developed some new power," Wesley said. "Or someone is using Chigger against us. That's more likely."

Billy worried that the pressure might harm his grandfather. He moved sideways so he could stand in front of the elder. Chigger focused his force in Billy's direction. Immediately the younger Buckhorn felt a hard, unseen wall come between him and his grandpa.

Billy resisted and pushed back against the force. Chigger quickly thrust his head toward Billy. This increased the pressure and pushed the teen to the floor.

"Ow!" Billy yelled as he landed on his wounded arm. The sound of Billy's yell seemed to disrupt the wall. This allowed Wesley to rush to his grandson.

"Are you all right?" the elder asked.

"I think I opened up a few stitches in my arm," Billy said as a red spot of blood spread across one of his bandages.

"This is more than a Night-Goer," Wesley said as he helped Billy to his feet. "We'll have to retreat and try to figure out what's at work here. Come on, let's get your arm looked after."

As Billy backed away from the bed, Wesley quickly grabbed his clear crystal and medicine pouch from the floor where they'd fallen. The two Buckhorns rushed from the room and closed the door.

After the intruders left his room, Chigger reached under his pillow. He found what he was looking for, the wonderful purple crystal he'd taken from the cave. It glowed as he stroked it. He'd grown very fond of it. It seemed to speak to him in a low whisper. It was more than a beautiful object. To him it was alive.

As he looked into the heart of the gem's center, he could somehow see for miles and miles. There was something there. Or someone. Chigger wasn't sure. But he felt a presence that had bonded with him. It was a stronger bond than friends or family. It was an ancient being that called to him. Holding the crystal tightly, he lay down. He pulled the covers over himself and the crystal so they could be together in the purple darkness. The boy drew his legs up close to his chest. He felt safe. Like a baby in his mother's womb.

Out in the living room, Wesley and Billy tried to breathe in deeply. The pressure in Chigger's room seemed to have cut off their oxygen for a while. Finally they could breathe easy.

"Is there someone you can call to come stay with you until your husband arrives?" Wesley asked Mrs. Muskrat. "You shouldn't be here alone."

"Why?" Chigger's mother asked. "What's going on?"

"I can't explain it all just yet," Wesley replied. "But we'll be back when we know more about what we're dealing with. In the meantime, get someone to stay with you, and don't allow your son to leave this house."

Wesley knew Chigger's mother was frightened and worried. But there was nothing he or Billy could do for her at the moment. The best thing for them to do next was figure out what had been let loose in the Cherokee Nation. That was the only way they'd be able to stop it.

They drove to Billy's dad's office at the college. They hoped he'd be in his office rather than in his classroom. Billy had already told his father about the markings he'd seen in the cave. The professor had been fascinated by his son's description. "Fascinating" seemed to be professor James Buckhorn's favorite word.

What was happening now had moved way beyond fascinating. What Billy, Wesley, Chigger, and the whole tribal nation were facing was a paranormal event beyond anyone's wildest nightmare. Billy and Wesley just had to convince the professor of this.

The professor's father and son arrived just as the professor was returning to his office from teaching a class. It was the first time both of them had ever shown up at his office at the same time.

"To what do I owe this unique visit?" he asked. The professor carried a large stack of student papers. "Wait a minute, young man," he said to Billy as he put the stack down on a chair near the door. "What are you doing out of bed?"

"We're here on urgent business," Wesley told his son. "And Billy is an important part of that business. You need to stop whatever it is you're doing and listen to what we have to say."

"Sounds serious," James said as he unlocked his office door. "Come inside."

He opened the door, picked up the stack of papers, and went inside. Wesley and Billy followed him in.

Billy always enjoyed going to his dad's office. One wall was lined from floor to ceiling with books on Native American topics. Another wall was covered with maps that showed where all the Indian tribes of North America lived. On a third wall hung a display of Cherokee masks, Plains Indian war shields, and other artifacts from Native tribes. It was a whole intertribal museum crammed into one small room.

Billy's father pushed an intercom button on his desk phone and a secretary answered.

"Yes, Professor Buckhorn," the woman's voice said.

"Please hold all my calls and move my student meetings to tomorrow," he said.

"Yes, sir," she replied and ended the call.

The professor's son and father began telling him what had been going on. The words came tumbling out of them like pieces of a jigsaw puzzle spilling out of a spilled puzzle box.

"Whoa, whoa, whoa," James said. "Slow down and put this story in some kind of order."

Wesley explained about the large number of people who'd been coming to see him for help. He told about the bats they'd seen. Billy described Chigger's situation and what he had done to them. Wesley showed his son the drawing of the Uktena in the *Cherokee Medicine Book*, and Billy revealed what he'd seen in that liquid at the bottom of the cavern.

"If I didn't already know and love you two, I'd think I was listening to a couple of kooks," the professor said when they'd finished their tale.

He then opened a drawer in his desk and pulled out a stack of opened books and computer printouts. He plopped the pile down on his desk.

"But, Billy, I listened when you first told me about that cave. The drawings and markings you found made me curious. I began doing some research."

He spread the books and papers out on the desk. Wesley and Billy leaned in to take a closer look at them. What they saw was a group of photos, drawings, and charts. These displayed aspects of the ancient Mound Builder cultures, buildings, and locations.

"Billy, I believe you and Chigger stumbled on the greatest archeology discovery of modern times," the professor said with a serious tone. "You know I'm not one to believe much in religious myths. But the things that have been happening to you got me thinking. What if there really is a core truth at the heart of tribal legends? What if some sort of ancient force has been let loose here in our state?"

A shock wave washed over Billy as those words sunk in. Could this be his own father saying these things? The man who only believed in what could be seen or touched? The man who only had faith in fact and science?

Billy and his grandpa had always assumed tribal legends and cultures had some truth to them at their roots. But now his father might think these ancient stories could contain a kernel of truth. Or may even be factually true.

"This is a welcome change of attitude," Wesley said in surprise.

"What do we do now?" Billy asked.

"Son, I think you and I should return to the cave," his father answered. "We'll bring the college archeology professor with us. We need to document the markings and drawings as soon as we can. Our Dr. Stevens is known the world over as the best digger in this state."

"Digger?" Billy asked. "What's a digger?"

"That's a nickname for archeologists," the professor replied, standing up. "They hate being called that. But everyone does it anyway."

He began restacking the papers and books as he spoke.

"Wesley, I suggest you call all the medicine people and stomp dance leaders together. They should be informed of what's going on. They need to know what they're up against. And maybe they can help you figure out how to help Chigger."

All three were silent for a moment as they realized what was happening and how crazy it all seemed.

"Time for the Buckhorns to swing into action," Wesley said finally.

CHAPTER 8
The Beast

Unknown to Billy, Wesley, or James, mysterious things had been happening in the area around that cave along the Arkansas River. Awinita was right. Something had come out of the cave with Billy and Chigger. And it wasn't just the bats.

After the helicopter had flown the wounded Billy to the hospital. And after a stranded Chigger had been picked up by his father. In the dark of night, the last remaining creature of its species had risen out of that murky liquid at the bottom of the cavern. The last surviving Horned Serpent, known to the Cherokees as Uktena, had slithered up that spiral pathway and out of its underground prison.

But Uktena wasn't the original name of that species. Other tribes at other times had known of the beast and called it other things. Tie-Snake, Crawfish Snake, and Great Snake were just a few. Each tribe had a name spoken in their language. Ancient stories of the creature and its strange powers had passed from father to son. Passed from tribe to tribe. All had been warned of its dangers. But those warnings were mostly long forgotten.

And now, for the first time in centuries, the creature's nostrils breathed in fresh air. His antlers felt the warming rays of the sun. For the first time in ages, his shimmering scales were able to feel fresh water. And for the first time in centuries, the muscles of his scaly body were able to stretch out to full length.

His scales were rejuvenated. His mind refreshed. His entire being free.

He flowed leisurely downstream. Down the Arkansas River. He wasn't concerned in the least that every living thing in his wake began to wither a little. They didn't die. They just became weakened. Every fish, lizard, plant, or mammal that came within twenty feet of him. What was actually happening was that a few years were being robbed from the ends of their lives. And those years were added to the life of the Uktena. This power was the very thing that Cherokee witches longed for. The Night-Goers and old Blacksnake learned their dark magic from the Horned Serpent.

And every creature that happened to gaze into the Uktena's eyes became dazed. Those dazed animals were unaware that the beast would soon devour them. Easy meals.

But the creature was missing his most prized possessions. The very things that provided his ultimate power were not in their places.

The brilliant diamond that once was fixed to his forehead had been stolen. And the dark crystal attached to the tip of his tail. It, too, had been removed. When the gems were returned to their rightful places, the beast would be fully restored.

The diamond would blaze forth with a brilliant, blinding light. The very sight of it could paralyze or kill a two-legged one. And the dark crystal contained loose pieces inside that rattled a warning whenever someone approached from behind. No one and no thing could catch him unaware.

The beast only had two weaknesses. And ages ago, the two-legged priests had learned one of them. They tricked him and lured him into a trap. They had spoken the powerful magic words that cast a spell on him. They caused him to sleep. That's when the crystal was removed from the tip of his tail.

Then the priests removed the diamond from his forehead. They must've known of its great power. That's why they kept it for themselves. The one called the Falcon Priest fixed it to the tip of his long staff. And the other Two-Leggeds worshipped him because he'd tamed the evil beast and imprisoned him in the dark lake.

Finally, while the beast was still asleep, they had transported him to the cave and sealed the doorway to his liquid prison. The Two-Leggeds knew the beast would remain close to the dark crystal. So they placed it on the pedestal to keep him within the lake.

But at long last, just a few days ago, the door had opened with a "psssst" sound. The creature waited until the two-legged intruders had left. He waited until the winged night-flyers had flown. With that prison door open and the dark crystal gone, he was free to roam the countryside once again.

Of course, he was still connected to those two gemstones, the white diamond and the dark crystal. He could feel their presence in the world. Especially the purple one. It was connected to him by an unseen force. Connected to his mind through invisible strings.

So as the two-legged intruders fled from the cave, the beast could feel the crystal leaving as well. He realized that the two-legged ones must've taken it with them. Oh, the anger and pain he'd suffered when he left the dark liquid. When he found the pedestal empty and the crystal gone.

With his eyes closed and his mind focused, he could feel it moving farther and farther from him. Until it came to rest a mere sixty miles to the north. The map in his mind told him where the crystal now resided. He didn't know the intruders called the place it was near Tahlequah. He'd never heard of the Cherokee Nation.

But he was able to mentally reconnect with the crystal and reattach those unseen strings. Whoever had it now would only hold it for a short while. For he would retrieve it in due time. All in due time.

For now he was content to float in the river, headed for a landmark he knew very well. It was a place the two-legged beings had built long ago. A place near the water with mounds that held the bones of their dead. A place that held the bones of a priest. This priest had been worshipped by his followers. Worshipped as part man and part god. Half bird and half man. The Falcon Priest.

He was the man who found out how to trick the beast and imprison him in that cave. When that man had died so many centuries ago, the white diamond on the top of that staff had been buried along with him.

What a glorious day it would be when the beast located that man's burial site. When he found those bones and scattered them to the winds. What a glorious day when, at long last, the stolen gem was once again fixed to the Horned Serpent's forehead.

That would be a day the world would remember. And regret.

CHAPTER 9
The Expedition

Back at the college, Billy's father was able to organize a trip to explore the cave on short notice. It wasn't hard to convince the head of the college to give Professor Buckhorn and Professor Stevens time off for the project. Finding and exploring an unknown site used by the Mound Builders would bring good publicity to the college. Professor Stevens got permission to bring along a young man named Doug, as well. Doug was a graduate student studying the ancient Indians of Oklahoma.

Two days later, the team of four headed south from the college. They drove a well-equipped college van and towed a boat trailer behind them. After driving a couple of hours, they decided to stop. A convenience store on the side of the road gave them a good place to go to the bathroom and buy snacks.

As he was paying for their goodies, Billy's dad saw the front page of a local newspaper. The headline read: "Parts of Ancient Mounds Destroyed by Unknown Vandal." Picking up the paper, he looked closely at the photo under the headline.

It showed that large holes had been dug into one of the mounds at Spiral Mounds State Park. These were ragged openings, not anything made with proper tools. And there was a strange path of withered plant life. It led from the river to the site.

"After exploring the cave, we'll have to check this out," James said. He handed the paper to Dr. Stevens as they headed back to the van.

They arrived at their destination about an hour later. It was a park area with a boat ramp on the Arkansas River. They put their gear in the boat and then put the boat in the river. They did a final check to make sure they had everything they needed. Then the team headed south down the river. They were following the same route Billy and Chigger had traveled.

"Here it is," Billy soon announced as they rounded the turn and came to the campsite used by the boys. Pointing upward, he added, "And there's the cave."

Quickly they unloaded the boats and made ready for their first cave entrance. Lights, cameras, tape measurers, pick hammers, and logbooks were items they placed in their backpacks.

The two professors and the graduate student were excited about what lay ahead. To them this was a chance to learn new information about the ancient peoples of the area. It could also make them celebrities in the world of diggers. That meant they could write books about their find and have their pictures published in magazines.

To Billy, however, this was much more. It was a journey into the deeper mysteries of life. An expedition into the supernatural side. A trip to the paranormal zone.

"Awinita, I need you to be with us today," he whispered while looking up at the cave. "Help us learn what we need to know for the good of our people and for Chigger." He gave a little nod to send his request on its way.

Awinita hadn't really told him what he needed to do to ask for her help, so he just did the best he could. No aroma of pie and cider reached his nose now.

Once inside the cave, each member of the team started performing his duty. Billy led the way with a powerful flashlight. The graduate student shot video as they went. Dr. Stevens took still pictures and jotted down notes. Billy's dad spoke into a small tape recorder. He described what they saw and experienced.

They reached the wall where the path separated into two. They examined and documented the markings and drawings etched into the stone.

"The half bird–half man figure is clearly a priest of the early Mound Builder culture," Billy's father said. "He would've led the people in ceremonies. He probably ruled their society. And this creature on the right looks like the Horned Serpent featured in several ancient cultures."

Then, as Billy and Chigger had done, the team first took the upward path. They were amazed by the beautiful crystal room that Billy took them to. And more amazed by the upper white crystal room. No one knew what the scenes on the walls were. Their meanings had been lost in the mists of time.

But their expedition continued. They photographed every step and every space within the upper and lower regions of the cave. When they finally made their way to the door at the bottom of the cavern, Dr. Stevens closely studied the markings on it.

"Fascinating," he said, just as Billy's father often did.

Billy showed them the pedestal where the dark crystal used to sit. He explained what happened when Chigger touched it. Peering through the open stone door, they examined the pool of dark liquid. They filled a test tube with a sample of the fluid. There were no signs of ripples or movement of any kind there.

And no signs of bats, either. The cave had been totally vacated.

"We need to find a language key," Dr. Stevens said. "That will allow us to decode the meaning of the markings on the door. They must be the symbols of an unknown language."

"That's fantastic," Billy's dad said. "Maybe they *are* part of an alphabet. This could be the oldest written Native language. This came way before Sequoyah invented the Cherokee system of writing in the early 1800s."

"Fascinating," Billy and the graduate student said together, mocking the older men. The younger two laughed, but the two professors didn't understand what was so funny.

"Well, we should wrap things up here and head to a motel for the night," Professor Buckhorn said. "Tomorrow we can get an early start to see what happened at the Mounds."

That evening, Professor Stevens used the motel's Wi-Fi network. He navigated to a research website used by colleges all over the country. The system's main computer memory was so large it could find the smallest bits of information on a topic. These bits were stored within huge collections at college libraries.

He pulled together the most recent discoveries of other diggers. People had been digging up ancient Native American sites for decades. What he found was, of course, fascinating. It was also very relevant to what his team had found in the cave that day.

"Two other archeologists have recently found symbols that look like the ones we found," Dr. Stevens said. "But these seem to appear only in the most secret chambers. These were places where the priests held private ceremonies. Most of the common people then couldn't read, write, or speak this language. Only the priests and medicine men could."

"That's like the Roman Catholic Church in medieval times," Billy's dad said. "All the church's services were held using the Latin language. Sermons were read by the priests from their Latin Bibles. None of the peasants could read it, write it, or speak it."

While the two professors carried on their discussion, Billy went to bed. That night, as he slept in the motel room, he began to dream. At first he was high atop a large, earthen mound. A building with a thatched roof stood on the mound's flat top. He looked out across the grassy meadow below the mound. There he saw hundreds of people looking up at him. He saw that these were American Indian people wearing simple clothing made of animal skins and natural materials.

The sound of their voices began to rise up to his ears. They were singing the haunting chant of a beautiful song. Then he looked down at his own body within the dream. He noticed he held a long wooden staff that had been carved. Images of plants and vines seem to grow up to the top of the staff. A large diamond-like gem was attached to the very top. It shone brilliantly in the noonday sun.

He walked to the edge of the mound top and held up the staff. That's when he saw that he was wearing a cape made of hawk or eagle feathers. The crowd below cheered. They seemed to adore him. He put the staff down. From the mound's edge, he leaped outward. Much to his surprise, he did not fall to the ground. He drifted out over the crowd.

Then he flew over them as they continued to cheer. Finally, the mound scene faded away. But Billy continued to fly across a changing landscape. The sun was setting in the west. It created a beautiful sight filled with billowy orange clouds. Soon his altitude dropped and he gently glided to the ground near a river. As he landed, he saw Grandma Awinita coming out from a cluster of nearby trees. Her thoughts reached his mind.

"Welcome, Grandson. This is my home in the spirit world. This is where you can find me whenever you need me."

Billy looked around at the beautiful setting. The sounds of the running water and the singing birds were very peaceful. But his mind was a jumble of worry and concern.

"I need you now," he said to her with his thoughts. "Chigger's in trouble. The Cherokee People are in trouble. And some sort of monster is on the loose."

"I know, I know," she said in a comforting tone. "All will be set right."

She led him to a tree stump near the river where he sat down. With her glowing energy and her thoughts, she calmed his mind and quieted his concerns. He was then able to enjoy that peaceful place.

"Tell Wesley that the purple crystal is the cause of Chigger's problems," she said. "The first thing that must be done is to get that object away from your friend. You'll call your grandpa as soon as you can to let him know."

She also revealed other things to him. But she said he would forget them when he woke up from this dream. The memory of these things would come back into his mind as he needed them.

"Is this a dream or is it really happening?" he asked when she'd finished.

"Both," she replied. "Sometimes that's just how the spirit world works."

CHAPTER 10
The Gathering

Meanwhile, Wesley had called together all the medicine men and women he knew. A meeting such as this had not been held in the Cherokee Nation in fifty years. Not since the 1960s when non-Native outsiders began using Native ceremonies for their purposes. These fake medicine men advertised their services and charged fees to an unaware public.

Now the Cherokee healers gathered at Live Oak Stomp Grounds. This was the place that Billy and Wesley went every Labor Day weekend. There they danced a healing dance all night.

The people who came to Wesley's meeting were mostly elders like him. There were a few younger ones scattered among them. But sadly, there weren't as many healers among the Cherokee Nation as there used to be.

After everyone had been cleansed in a traditional ceremony, they sat in the seven arbors facing the central square. This was where everyone normally danced during the all-night stomp dance in a spiral around the central fire. Wesley stepped out into the square to speak.

"I'll get right to the reason for this gathering," he said, speaking in the Cherokee language. "How many of you are treating more people than you normally do?" Almost everyone raised their hands. A murmur of chatters spread through the crowd.

"And how many of those people have been seeing bats near their homes?" he asked. Again, almost everyone raised their hands. The chatter became louder as the healers realized they all faced similar problems.

"And are these folks getting better after your treatments?" Wesley asked. "Are they being healed by traditional methods?" One very loud "No" after another rang out from the group. The chatter among the healers burst loudly across the dance grounds.

"All right, all right," Wesley said in English, trying to calm everyone down. He waited for them to settle.

"That's why we're here," he said, continuing in English. "So we can look at what we are facing. So we can try to understand what's causing this strange sickness among our people."

And so a working discussion began among these people. They were, after all, the most experienced in such matters. These matters were beyond science—beyond health clinics, doctors' offices, and hospitals. These matters were of the paranormal realms.

So this group learned that something very unusual was happening, unusual even for them. Something more than regular symptoms was coming forth. And what was needed was more than everyday remedies. What would be required of them now was of a higher order. Greater effort and greater power were called for.

Wesley listened carefully to the ideas that came from the healers at that gathering. And after the talks were over, he asked three people to stay a little while longer. These three had come up with some of the best ideas that day.

The first was a tall, older Cherokee man named Elwood. He lived in the eastern part of the Nation. The second was a short, middle-aged Indian from down south named Chester. The third was an attractive elderly woman named Wilma. She lived near the city of Tulsa. Through the years, Wesley had heard many good things about all three. He knew he could trust them.

After everyone else had left, he told these healers about a special case he needed their help with. All of them had offered to do anything they could to be of service. So he told them about Chigger. Wesley hoped that the power the four of them had might be able to break through to Chigger. Whatever it was that formed the barrier around the boy needed strong medicine to melt it away. After they heard what Wesley was up against, all three agreed to help him. They planned to make their move the very next day.

Early the next morning, Wesley got a phone call from Billy.

"Billy, how's the exploration going?" Wesley asked. He was glad to hear from his grandson. "Find out anything yet?"

"Last night in a dream, Grandma told me that Chigger's problem comes from the dark crystal he took out of the cave."

"I'm so jealous and at the same time happy that you get to see Grandma," Wesley said.

"She told me you'd be feeling that way," Billy said. "She also told me to remind you that I had to get struck by lightning and die in the hospital to be able to see her."

"Good point," he laughed. "I'll try to remember that."

"The first thing you have to do is get the crystal away from Chigger," his grandson continued. "That won't be easy because the Uktena is connected to the crystal. That means he's also connected to Chigger." Billy actually didn't remember that piece of information from his dream. It just popped out of his mouth.

"Oh no," Wesley said with sadness. "Who would ever think we'd be dealing with the old Horned Serpent in our time?"

"Yeah, who?" Billy asked seriously. "Please don't hurt Chigger," he added after a pause.

"Of course not," his grandpa answered. "We only have Chigger's best interest in mind."

"We'll be down here one more day and then back home," Billy added.

"Remember this," Wesley said. "If you come across the beast, don't look into his eyes."

"Ah, yes—good reminder," he said. "Thanks, Grandpa. Gotta go."

When Billy was off the phone, Professor Stevens gathered the team for an early morning breakfast at a cafe near their motel. Overnight he had done a simple test on the dark liquid sample he had collected from the cave.

"It appears to be nothing more than a strong herbal tea," he said. "It's like a tea you might take at night to make you sleepy. But this stuff is strong enough to put a horse to sleep."

Billy thought about that for a moment.

"It sounds like one of Grandpa's herbal remedies," he commented. "Something he gives a patient who's having trouble sleeping. Maybe a medicine man put it in the water."

"When I get back to the lab at the college, I can do a more thorough test," Stevens said as he took his last bite of eggs. "Then I can tell you exactly what the herb is."

"Okay, team. Time to hit the road," Billy's dad announced. "We're due at Spiral Mounds in a few minutes. The park is just down the road."

The four-member team climbed into their van and headed out.

At about the same time, the four healers, led by Wesley, headed to Chigger's mobile home. Armed with the new information from Billy, they hoped they'd be successful.

Chigger's father, Sam, answered the door when they arrived. He'd come right home from his out-of-town job after his wife had called. The tall Cherokee man invited the four medicine people into his humble home. He had never really believed much in traditional Cherokee medicine. But his son needed help from someone, and they were the only ones offering.

Chigger's mother sat on the couch in her bathrobe. Her hair was a mess. She was a mess.

"That's not my boy in there," she said, pointing to Chigger's bedroom. "Something or someone has taken him over. That's the only thing that can explain it."

"He hasn't eaten any of the food we've given him in days," Chigger's father added. "He just throws it at us and curses. He keeps demanding raw meat, but I'm not going to give that to him."

"If you'll allow it, we'd like to go in and check on Chigger," Wesley told the distressed parents. "Just to see if we can do any good."

Sam nodded his permission. He then sat down on the couch next to his wife.

Outside Chigger's bedroom, Wesley spoke to his band of healers.

"Remember," he whispered. "As soon as we enter, take up your positions in the four directions. Hopefully that will prevent him from being able to focus and put up the wall."

They nodded their agreement, and Wesley quietly opened the door. The room smelled of rotting food and worse. They tiptoed in. Chigger was standing in the middle of his bed. In his hands was the glowing purple crystal.

"Billy was right," Wesley whispered loudly. "The crystal from the cave has got some power over the boy. We've got to get it away from him."

Chigger looked up from the crystal. The healers fanned out around him in the room. That's when he began speaking in tongues, speaking a language no one in the room could understand. His bloodshot eyes opened wide. His head rolled in a circle as he spoke the angry gibberish.

At a signal from Wesley, the four moved in on the crazed teenager. When he could no longer see everyone at the same time, he panicked. At that point Chigger's body jerked in a spasm and he fell back on the bed.

"Hold him down while I grab the crystal!" Wesley yelled.

Pulling a tanned leather bag from his pocket, Wesley used the bag to pry the crystal from Chigger's hands. The elder did not want to come into direct contact with the gem. It might attach itself to him.

That's when Wesley saw the burnt, raw flesh on the palms of Chigger's hands for the first time. It must have been very painful to hold, but Billy's friend would not loosen his grip on the smooth stone. Then Wesley got an idea.

"Keep holding him down," he told the others and left the room.

"Do you have some raw meat in your refrigerator?" Wesley asked the Muskrats back in the living room.

"Yes, we do," Mrs. Muskrat said. "I was planning on making a couple of steaks for dinner."

"Good," Wesley replied. "Please bring me one of them. And hurry!"

"You're not going to give it to him, are you?" Sam asked. "I don't think that's a good idea."

"I'm going to distract him with it so we can get that crystal away from him," the elder assured him. "In the meantime, please call the hospital and get an ambulance here as quickly as you can."

Molly ran to the kitchen and took an uncooked steak out of the fridge while Sam picked up the phone to call the hospital.

"This won't take too long," Wesley said as he carried the meat toward the bedroom.

Back inside Chigger's bedroom, Wesley approached the bed.

"Look what I've got for you," he said to Chigger. He hoped to attract the creature that was somehow connected to the boy.

Chigger stopped struggling against the three people who were holding him. He looked over at Wesley. When the boy saw the meat, he tried to sit up and reach for it with his mouth.

"If you want it, you'll have to grab it with your hands," Wesley taunted.

He sniffed the meat for dramatic effect.

Wesley stood holding the raw steak at the edge of the bed. The three healers held the boy tightly so he couldn't reach the meat with his mouth. Chigger had to consider his situation seriously for a moment. Which did he want more, the crystal or the steak? He had a powerful craving for the meat, but the purple gem cried out to be held closely to his chest.

During that long moment, Elwood prepared the leather bag that would hold the crystal.

Finally, Chigger's hunger won out. He released the crystal from his burnt hands. Wilma, who was closest to the boy, grabbed the gem using the bedspread as a buffer.

Elwood held the bag open as she stuffed it inside. Chester continued to restrain Chigger.

Wesley allowed Chigger to grab the meat in his bare hands. The boy immediately screamed in pain as his burns touched the meat. He dropped the steak and looked down at his scorched hands. That's when he realized he no longer held his precious crystal.

He cried out in agony. He thrashed about against those who held him.

"Sam, come quick!" Wesley yelled, hoping to be heard over Chigger's yelps.

Mr. Muskrat ran into the room, eyes wide with fear. What was happening to his boy?

"Help hold your son down on the bed and talk to him," Wesley said. "Maybe if he hears his father's voice, the real Chigger will start to come back to the surface."

"The ambulance is on the way," Sam said as he took his son's arms in his hands. He began talking to him in a soft voice. It hurt the man to see the burns all over his son's hands. But he kept speaking to him in a calm tone.

Wesley took the leather pouch out the front door and placed it in the bed of his pickup. He would hide the dark crystal in the woods behind his house until he learned what needed to happen next. He hoped Billy already knew what to do or would soon find out.

CHAPTER 11

The Falcon Priest

Soon the ambulance arrived at the Muskrat home. The emergency medical team had never seen someone in Chigger's condition. He was half starved. He had third-degree burns on the palms of his hands. But these pros worked quickly to get the boy on a gurney and into their vehicle. Then they sped off toward the hospital.

Outside the mobile home, Wesley thanked Wilma, Chester, and Elwood for their assistance. The four healers went their separate ways. But not before Wilma had slipped a note into Wesley's hand.

"When things settle down, I'd like to have you over to my place for dinner," the note read. Wilma's phone number was written at the bottom. Wesley looked up and blushed as the woman drove out of the Muskrats' driveway. With a smile, he placed the note in his wallet. *To be continued*, he thought. Awinita had told him over and over again to find someone.

Meanwhile, the expedition team had arrived at Spiral Mounds State Park. They spoke to the park's director, Peter Langford. He had agreed to meet them when he learned that the famous Dr. Stevens was a member of the team.

Langford said the damage had been done a couple of nights ago, and the trail left by the vandals came from the river. He showed the team the strange trail of withered plant life. It led from the river into the park. What had caused this trail was a complete mystery to everyone who'd seen it.

"But what's really strange is what happened to our night watchman," Langford said. "He says he was making his midnight rounds through the park. He heard digging, scraping, and grunting noises from the mound I'm going to show you."

"So he was able to catch the vandals in the act?" Billy's father asked.

"That's what's so strange," Langford replied. "The watchman claims to have turned on his flashlight when he arrived at the mound. All he saw for a brief second was a pair of large, glowing eyes. And there was a bright reflection from those eyes. It sent the light back to him in a flash. He went blind and became paralyzed. Isn't that the craziest thing you've ever heard?"

"Were they like snake eyes?" Billy asked. "You know, with a narrow vertical pupil?"

Langford was stunned by Billy's description.

"What would make you say that?" Langford asked. "That's exactly how the guard described them, but I dismissed his description as the ravings of a man gone mad."

"Is he all right? Can we speak to him?" Billy's father asked. "Whatever he heard or saw before going blind could be useful to us."

"I guess I could give him a call when we get back to the office," Langford said. "But first I'll show you the damage to the mound."

No archeology work had been done around the mound site since the 1950s. At that time the diggers decided to delay any further digging until new methods and better equipment had been invented. They were sure that the last mound contained very valuable artifacts and human remains. They wanted to leave those things undisturbed. Now the park, which was open daily to the public, was closed because of the damage.

"There was another disturbing thing about the whole incident," Langford said. "The damage was done to the least publicly known mound."

Langford continued to talk as he led the team toward that mound.

"Only a small, select group of scientists even knew that there was still one mound waiting to be explored."

"That decision was made to prevent exactly what has now happened," Dr. Stevens confirmed. "We hoped that illegal pottery hunters wouldn't break into the park and dig up the place. That's what happened back in the 1930s and 1940s. So I must ask how anyone knew where to dig."

The group had almost reached the mound when Billy's dad spoke.

"This must be the burial mound that held the bones and objects belonging to the leaders of this community," he said.

"The Falcon Priest," Billy blurted out. "He would've been buried here."

Langford, Stevens, and Billy's father just stared at the young man. How did he know this? Their question would have to wait. They now saw firsthand the damage done to the burial mound.

A huge, ragged hole had been gouged out of the side of the mound. Dried human bones, broken pieces of pottery, and cracked parts of stone statues were scattered about.

"My god," Dr. Stevens exclaimed. "This is a disaster."

As the digger and the professor examined the scattered fragments, Billy peered into the gaping hole. Intuition told him that something important was still inside the mound. Something had been overlooked during the frantic search. The searcher was interrupted by the guard in the dark of night.

Billy stepped into the hole in the mound, not knowing what he'd find. He saw stone and bone pieces sticking out of shredded dirt. But a long, tube-like object caught his eye. It was partly buried and partly sticking out at the back of the hole.

Scraping the debris away from the object, he could see it was a container. It was made of thick, round river cane. Carefully, he pulled it away from the dirt and brushed it off. He carried it outside the mound and laid it down on the ground.

Langford noticed what Billy was doing and reacted.

"Nothing should be touched or taken from the mound," he said angrily. He stomped over to where Billy stood.

"He is a member of my team," Dr. Stevens said loudly. "As such, he's allowed to examine anything that's already been disturbed by the vandals. We have to find out how much damage has been done."

He moved quickly and stood between Billy and the park director.

"Of course," Langford said as he backed down. "You are right."

"I think now would be a good time for you to contact the night watchman," Billy's father told the park director.

"Right again," Langford replied. "I'll see you gentleman back at my office later."

The team waited until the man was out of sight before doing anything else. Then Dr. Stevens handed Billy a pair of latex gloves to put on. Then he stooped down to see what Billy had found. With gloved hands, Billy carefully opened one end of the hollow tube.

Dr. Stevens pointed his flashlight into the tube, but he couldn't make out what was inside.

"I'll pick up the tube and tilt it slightly so the contents can slide out," he said to Billy. "You catch whatever's inside. Be very careful."

Then the digger, who was already wearing gloves, tilted the tube. A long, straight wooden rod began sliding out. Wrapped around the rod was a collection of feathers. They had been tied or sewn together.

"Doug, spread out that sheet of plastic so we can lay this down and unroll it," Dr. Stevens instructed the grad student.

Once the plastic was down, Billy and Dr. Stevens unrolled the feather-covered rod. The teen couldn't believe what he was seeing. The objects had been hidden away in that tube for centuries. First there was the feathered cape he'd been wearing in his dream. Then there was the staff he'd been holding in that dream. At the top of the staff was the brilliant diamond he'd seen as he stood on the tall mound in front of hundreds of people.

"It's the Falcon Priest's cape and staff," Billy said.

"How do you know that?" the digger asked the teen.

"I was wearing this cape and holding this staff in my dream last night," Billy said. "I stood on top of a large, flat-top mound. I think I *was* the Falcon Priest in that dream."

"So much of what we know about these ancient people is based on educated guesses," Dr. Stevens said. "So how is it that you seem to know specific details about the Mound Builders?"

"You wouldn't believe me if I told you," Billy answered. "As a matter of fact, I don't expect you to believe anything I say. You go ahead and work with your best guesses. I'm on this expedition for a totally different reason than you are."

Dr. Stevens looked at Billy's father with a puzzled look.

"Billy's right," Professor Buckhorn said. "You have your tasks, and Billy has his. I'm here to coordinate both efforts."

Dr. Stevens had no reply.

"So, Professor, explain to me how this cape and staff have been preserved so well all these hundreds of years," Billy's father asked. He wanted to change the subject.

As the digger began his explanation, Billy started to hear buzzing in his ears. This was the same buzzing noise he heard a few days ago when Awinita introduced him to Uncle Luther.

Billy tuned out Dr. Stevens as he focused on the buzzing.

"It's me again," Awinita's voice said from within the buzz. "I've got someone else for you to meet."

"I hope it's not another long-lost uncle," Billy thought to himself and then laughed.

CHAPTER 12
Enough for Now

"No uncle this time," Awinita communicated. "But he might be a very distant relative." As Billy watched, his grandma appeared in her glowing form inside the hole in the mound. Slowly coming into view beside her was a tall, majestic Native American man. Billy was pretty sure no one else saw them.

"I've combed the far reaches of the spirit world to find him," Awinta said. "Here stands before you the original Falcon Priest, with knowledge he wishes to share with you."

Billy tried as best he could to focus on the spirit man's glowing outline. But the ancient spirit drifted in and out of view. He was barely able to adjust himself to the physical world.

"It's been a thousand years since he tried to interact with the world of the living," Awinita said to Billy, "so be patient."

"The markings on the beast's prison door at the bottom of the cave are indeed those of our sacred language," the man said. "What is written there are the words that must be spoken in order to recapture the serpent and hold him in that prison."

"How will we ever be able to speak those words?" Billy asked. "We do not have that knowledge. We don't know your language."

"When the time comes, I will speak them through you," he replied. "But there are many steps that must be taken before that can happen."

"What are they?"

"First the dark crystal must be returned to its place near the door. And the person who removed it must be the one who replaces it. Then the bearer of the cape and the staff must find the Horned Serpent. Only the rightful new Falcon Priest will be protected from the beast's harmful powers. And only if that priest is wearing the cape and holding the staff.

"When the creature sees the gem within that staff, he will become hypnotized. The gem on the staff is the very stone that was once on his own forehead. He will follow it wherever it goes. You must lead him back into the cave and lure him back into the pit. Once he's entered the medicine lake, the words on the door have to be spoken. When the final word is spoken, the door will close and reseal itself. It's all very simple."

Ha! Billy thought. *Simple for you, maybe.*

"I will be ready when Awinita contacts me," the man said. "I will appear where you are. I will speak the words through you. I will use your physical body, your voice. Then the creature will be safely secure once more."

The glowing man began to fade at that point.

"Wait," Billy pleaded. "I have so many questions to ask you. Where did the beast come from in the first place? How did you trap him and imprison him?"

The man continued to fade and soon was gone.

"I'm sorry, Billy," Awinita said. "That's all for now. You should return home to visit with Chigger and Wesley. They will have parts to play in conquering the creature. Good-bye for now."

She, too, faded away, leaving Billy with many unanswered questions. Many worries and concerns. Many loose ends to tie up.

The expedition team worked at the site the rest of the day. Dr. Stevens wanted to inventory the artifacts and remains that had been damaged. Then he wanted to make plans for a future dig there.

But all Billy could think about was the whole fantastic string of events that had unfolded over the past couple of weeks. Was this just a series of freak accidents or was it a sign of the future? Was he in the middle of a return to the days of miracles and monsters? This had been predicted in some tribal legends. He inwardly checked his own intuition on the matter. This is what Grandpa

Wesley encouraged him to. He didn't like what his intuition was telling him.

At the end of the day, the team loaded their equipment back in the van. Billy took this time to speak to his father in private. He wasn't sure his father would believe him, but the teen told his dad about the visit from the spirit of the Falcon Priest earlier that day.

"At some point Wesley, Chigger, you, and I will have to return to that cave with the dark crystal and reseal the Horned Serpent in the lake," Billy said. "And I will need to be wearing the falcon cape and holding the priest's staff."

"I was afraid you were going to say that," his father replied. "This has all become more real than I'd like to admit. Nothing surprises me anymore when it comes to the things that happen in your life."

"Same goes for me," Billy confirmed. "I feel more abnormal than ever."

"You and I and Grandpa will have to talk more about this later," Billy's dad said. He put a comforting hand on his son's shoulder.

"For now, I don't think we should mention anything to Stevens about you needing to have the cape and staff. He'll probably have a major meltdown over it."

During the drive back to Tahlequah, Dr. Stevens and his grad student sat in the front of the van. They talked a mile a minute about their new discoveries. Billy and James, sitting in the van's middle row, were mostly silent. Mr. Buckhorn tried a couple of times to get Billy talking about everyday subjects. He brought up how much school Billy had missed. And asked how he and Sara were doing.

But Billy had no interest or energy for such things. His mind was focused on whether or not his best friend would get well and be his old self again. Would Wesley and the other medicine people of the tribe be able to rid the Nation of these troubles? Was he, sixteen-year-old Billy Buckhorn, somehow linked to the Falcon Priest? That's what his dream and the words of the spirit priest seemed to mean.

Extreme fatigue overtook him as the van rambled across the landscape. The sun set in the western sky. And out of nowhere, the sweet smell of apple cider and pumpkin pie reached his nostrils. This put his mind at ease. It told him everything would eventually be all right. Even with all the unanswered questions floating through his mind, that was enough for now.

He slept a dreamless sleep the rest of the way home.

ACKNOWLEDGMENTS

I would like to thank Jesse and Sandy Hummingbird for reviewing this manuscript and contributing to the development of this book. They provided useful feedback regarding the way aspects of Cherokee culture and medicine practices are used.

I also want to thank my best friend and significant other, Lola, for her love and support in all things. She has been by my side for more than ten years. I love and appreciate her so much. No words printed here could really express my true feelings, but I couldn't do this work without her with me.

ABOUT THE AUTHOR

Gary Robinson, a writer and filmmaker of Cherokee and Choctaw Indian descent, has spent more than twenty-five years working with American Indian communities to tell the historical and contemporary stories of Native people in all forms of media. His television work has aired on PBS, Turner Broadcasting, Ovation Network, and others. His nonfiction books, *From Warriors to Soldiers* and *The Language of Victory*, reveal little-known aspects of American Indian service in the US military from the Revolutionary War to modern times. He has also written three other teen novels, *Thunder on the Plains*, *Tribal Journey*, and *Little Brother of War*, and two children's books that share aspects of Native American culture through popular holiday themes: *Native American Night Before Christmas* and *Native American Twelve Days of Christmas*. He lives in rural central California.